STORM FRONT

AN UNWELCOMED ARRIVAL

Joanna Bright Dungeness Bay Mysteries

BOOK 1

KIT CRUMB

Storm Front - An Unwelcomed Arrival
Joanna Bright Dungeness Bay Mysteries – Book 1

By Kit Crumb

Owl Creek Press
Ashland, Oregon 97520
owlcreekpress@gmail.com
kitcrumb.com

Cover design: Chris Molé - booksavvystudio.com

ISBN: 978-0-9906068-7-1

To Chris

Prologue

DUNGENESS BAY, OREGON

Thayer Spelling walked the beach below the prominent China bluff for the hundredth time. She paused to watch the waves crash on the rocks beyond the beach, to gaze up at China bluff, so named for the Chinese apothecary that looked down on the surf. She felt that her assignment to Dungeness Bay was like being sent to Moose Jaw, Alaska. Her publisher had handed her the outline for a documentary and the promise of a hefty advance if she could bring back a story. At 74, Thayer was the oldest in the stable of writers represented by Portland-based Beach Front Publishing.

When she had arrived, the mayor had met her at the bus station, excited at the prospect of a documentary about the history of his town. When the publisher contacted him, she said they were sending their most senior writer. His image of a Lois Lane or Erin Brockovich vanished when a woman in her middle seventies stepped off the bus. Thayer laughed at the memory of the look on his face. He'd taken her on a tour of the tiny coastal town.

Thayer opened the story with the 1882 exclusion act, signed by President Chester A. Arthur, that restricted the Chinese from owning or operating a business, then blended in the influx of miners and the timber industry that eventually drove out most of the Chinese. She highlighted how those that remained created a small community that depended on the two practitioners of Chinese medicine who worked out of an apothecary and herb shop. During the tour, it had come up again and again from the locals and even from the mayor himself that the old apothecary had been spared the wrecking ball for its historic value, and, almost as an afterthought, the story of hidden gold had swirled around the structure. She dismissed the idea of hidden gold as a story concocted to attract tourists.

For the sake of the story, she didn't complain about the conditions of the Apothecary, but the apartment above, where she was expected to live, was a dump. Thayer immediately contacted her editor, Kindle Martin, about the conditions she would have to endure and was wired the funds necessary to upgrade the bathroom only to the 21st century. The Apothecary was dusty to the point of being filthy, with dozens of shelves lined with bottles and boxes labeled in both Mandarin and Cantonese that no one could read. There was no phone, and the structure had no cell service. To top it off, Thayer didn't drive, yet had planned to conduct her interviews in town at the tiny library. The saving grace came when the mayor dropped her off and said he would send someone to take her to town. His name was Gus Hasselbacker, a Gulf War vet who walked with a reminder of his service aided by a cane, whose grandfather was an aging miner who survived the 1918 flu epidemic thanks to the two Chinese doctors who had worked at the apothecary. Gus was also her first interview and, as her story took shape, a sounding board.

Thayer interviewed the children, grandchildren, and sometimes great-grandchildren of the founders of Dungeness Bay. Tales of miners coming to the Chinese doctors for issues ranging from gout and dysentery to the more serious like pneumonia, and how they paid with gold, gold dust, and cash were abundant. She began to take the folktale of hidden gold more seriously when her research revealed no evidence of any gold from the apothecary ever being assayed. Her conclusion was that taking any cash to a bank or gold to an assay office would have been an indication that the doctors were operating a business. They would have been shut down.

She kept her conclusions to the whereabouts of the gold separate from the body of the story but confided in Gus that the gold was located in one of three places. Because of a fear of being burned out of business by anti-Chinese factions, two of the locations were away from the premises the third was within the apothecary.

Thayer checked her watch. She had three interviews lined up for the afternoon. This would give her just enough time to check out two of the three possibilities. The switchbacks made climbing to the top of the bluff longer but less steep. She paused briefly at the Chinese cemetery, then continued past the apothecary and parking area to the narrow trail that led to the stone smokehouse and root cellar. She wanted to check her best hunch first and pushed through the smokehouse door. Just as described by numerous interviewees was the plank floor. With a determined effort, she pried up the first plank, which loosened the remaining planks. There were no windows and the pit below the planks was dark. She cursed herself for not bringing a flashlight, then heard someone approach. She turned and stepped just beyond the pit.

"Oh, it's you."

She never saw what struck her on the side of the head, and was dead even before she crumpled, falling backward into the pit.

Slowly, methodically, the floor was replaced, the final plank fit tight, hiding the body of Thayer Spelling from prying eyes.

STORM FRONT

An Unwelcomed Arrival

Chapter One

Joanna Bright stepped into the street and gazed at the house that overlooked Stewart's cove, her house, but no longer her home, not since the passing of her beloved husband, K. C., of 30 years. It wasn't yet nine o'clock, and up the street at the Tor House, once the home of poet Robinson Jeffers, the parking lot was already filling with tourists. She laughed at the sight and knew she was making the right decision to leave the Monterey peninsula.

She stepped onto the front lawn of the only home she'd known since she was twenty-two, straightened the for sale sign, and paused to take in the hedges and plants she'd nurtured over the past three decades. Was it crazy to leave these memories behind for a new start? After all, she was fifty-two, and now a widow. She walked to the side of the house where she and K. C. had watched dozens of pelicans cross the bay a hundred times, only now she was alone.

She turned at the sound of cars and sighed. It hadn't always been like this, all the tourists, all the traffic.

She'd come to Monterey in 1979, single, twenty, and so idealistic, thinking that she could make a living from her art. In a one-room studio over a garage, she had dreams of getting her art into one of the famous Carmel studios. Joanna shook her head and wiped at her eyes. She'd made that dream come true and now she was leaving it behind. She felt an inner satisfaction at the decision but wanted to cry.

At twenty-two, she'd met K. C. Bright, a successful entrepreneur thirteen years her senior. He'd introduced her to a creative circle of people who took her in and whom she soon became friends with a carpenter, a surfer, and some holdouts from the 1967 Monterey pop festival—free spirits all. She and K. C. married in 1981, and he built this house overlooking Stewart's Cove. Over the years, many of their friends moved away, some south to Big Sur, others north to

San Francisco. She and K. C. had talked about moving somewhere and leaving the tourists behind, but they couldn't bear the idea of leaving the cove and peninsula.

With a heavy heart, Joanna climbed into K. C.'s aging pickup. She'd sold the Fiat and their cherished Austin-Healey. She backed out of the driveway for what she knew was the last time, and closed her mind off to all the memories, at least for now. The clock on the dashboard, in bold green numbers, indicated nine o'clock. She had an appointment with their attorney—now her attorney—Ned Branch, at 9:30. He'd been part of that creative circle, all those years ago, perhaps a little more ambitious. Ned had left the peninsula, gone to college, and returned, hanging out his shingle in Pacific Grove: N. Branch, attorney-at-law.

Now all she had to do was fight her way through traffic and find parking as close to his office as she could get. Pacific Grove was almost as hazardous with tourists as Monterey and Carmel.

"What luck," Joanna said as she watched a car pull out of a spot directly in front of Ned's law office. "And early too."

She picked up the want ad she'd cut out of the paper and the printout from the ad's link. *Wanted, a Docent/Caretaker for a small museum on the Oregon Coast. For photos and contact information, go to the link at the bottom of this ad.*

She flipped back the stapled copy of the ad and read the printout out loud.

"The Kam Wa Chung Company was an apothecary set up by Kam Wa Chung in 1888 to provide traditional Chinese medicine to the many Chinese who fished and crabbed the area, and local miners and town folk. When Doc Hay, as Ing Hay was known to the locals, passed away in 1928, he deeded the building and its contents to the newly formed village, Dungeness Bay. But as fishing and crabbing gave way to the timber industry, the building was abandoned. In 1967, when China Bluff, the location of the apothecary, was being surveyed for a park, it was discovered that the building was owned by the city. Now the apothecary is a popular museum, and we're looking for the right person to serve as docent/caretaker." Joanna paused and looked up. "That would be me." She closed her eyes and rationalized that the move to Dungeness Bay would work out because an apartment above the museum and a small stipend would be provided.

She was sure that her thirty years of tai chi and chi kung, her single status, and her degree as a physical therapist had swayed the city council's decision to hire her.

Joanna opened her eyes; this was the second time her knowledge of tai chi and chi kung had factored into her life. She pressed the ad against her chest and allowed a memory to surface. During the troubled years when she and K. C. found out that they couldn't have children, tai chi, and especially chi kung, had kept her grounded.

A knocking at the window brought her around.

"Earth to Joanna; are you okay?"

She opened the door and slid into the warm embrace of Ned Branch.

"My nine o'clock left early, and I saw you sitting out here." He looked past her at the suitcases in the bed of the truck. "Taking a trip?"

"I'm leaving the peninsula Ned."

Taking her hand, he led her away from the pickup. "Let's go inside and talk."

Ned's law office was on the second floor of a two-story building once owned by the Wu Tung Company, an organization that oversaw profits made by Chinese laborers. Built in the 1900s, it faced Pacific Grove's main drag and was conveniently next to the post office. There was no elevator, and the two trudged up the stair in silence.

Ned's office was a twenty-by-twenty space with an oak desk in the middle. The walls were adorned with pictures of Monterey and Carmel before the onslaught of tourists.

Ned pulled an overstuffed wingback chair from a corner to the front of his desk for Joanna.

"K. C. left you a hefty inheritance and you sold your physical therapy business for a bundle, so I know money's not an issue. I assumed that you would relocate somewhere in Carmel Valley."

"Look at the pictures on the wall, Ned, then take a walk along Ocean Avenue or just drive down to Big Sur, maybe the Bixby Bridge. K. C. is gone, and aside from you, so are most of our friends, and certainly the special ambiance of living on the Monterey Peninsula. I'm fifty-two years old," Joanna said, taking a deep breath. She could already feel her eyes burn, "there's nothing left for me here."

"Exactly, you're a fifty-two-year-old woman who's alone. Where are you going to go?"

"Don't be a chauvinist Ned, you're better than that. Besides, I have a destination and a position waiting for me."

"Forgive me, Joanna, I'm just concerned." He looked down at his desk blotter and then back up into the moist eyes of his long-time friend. "What destination? You're going back to work?"

"Not work, exactly. I'm headed north to Oregon and the coastal town of Dungeness Bay. I'll work at a museum there—a Chinese apothecary dating back to the turn of the century, and completely preserved. The city council has offered me the living quarters above the museum and a small stipend."

Ned swiveled his chair around so he could face his computer, and Googled Dungeness Bay.

"Located in Bay County." He looked over at Joanna. "One of the smallest counties in the state, hit hard with budget cuts. Population two thousand four hundred and eighty-eight. Founded in 1889 as the crabbing capital of the Pacific Northwest. Are you serious?"

"I'm not here to argue Ned. I'd like you to connect with the town bank, open an account for me, and transfer all my funds."

"You want me to close out your Monterey account? You *are* serious. Why don't I leave it open in the event that you decide to move back?"

"I have no intention of moving back." She mentally flashed back on how she'd struggled to make peace with the idea of leaving so much behind. "I made this appointment to say goodbye to an old friend," Joanna said and stood. "Now get around here, give me a hug, and wish me safe travels. I've got a nine-hour drive. The Dungeness Bay city council has arranged a welcome dinner at the Whalers Inn and Restaurant."

Ned stood, walked around the desk, wrapped Joanna's five-foot-eleven-inch frame in a bear hug, and then stepped back. "Safe travels. Call me any time, day or night. I'll always be here for you."

CHAPTER TWO

Fifty miles off the Oregon coast, black storm clouds gathered, pulled, and pushed toward land by a sixty-five-mile-an-hour wind.

Joanna left Crescent City, California, crossed into Oregon, slowed at the sight of the storm clouds gathering on the horizon, and pulled onto the shoulder of Highway 101. She climbed out of the cab, battered by the wind, and pulled the cover closed over the bed of the Chevy pickup, protecting her suitcases in case it rained.

She passed the tiny town of Waldport and the Seal Rock tourist attraction. Joanna was just one hundred miles south of Dungeness Bay when the storm hit land. She could feel the old truck rock in the wind, and despite it being mid-afternoon, it appeared much darker. Rain soon splashed off her windshield in giant drops, making her glad she'd stopped earlier to cover her things in the back. As she drove along, she kept increasing the cadence of the windshield wipers to keep pace with the downpour. When it got so dark that she turned on her lights, she checked her watch and began nervously talking to herself.

"Wow. Welcome to the Oregon Coast."

When a gust of wind hit her head-on, Joanna felt the big V8 engine pulling, then shifting down.

"This wind is something else," she whispered and reached behind the passenger seat, feeling around for her coat, wishing she'd unpacked her windbreaker. She rolled into Dungeness Bay ahead of schedule. "I'll check out the apothecary then head over to Whalers Inn."

She reached over to the passenger seat and fished past the paper maps of the Oregon Coast, the box of tissues, and under her cell phone until she found the directions for the museum. When she passed the Outpouring coffee shop, the gas station,the bookstore, and the hardware store, she was surprised that they were all closed. The center of town was marked by the town's only traffic light, held almost horizontal by the wind.

"The first left after the light. The museum must be right on the coast," she recited as she made the turn.

Less than a mile later, the road became gravel, lined with tall red alder and poplar trees. She parked directly in front of the apothecary. The museum was two stories, but the lower portion was constructed of stone twenty feet high, and in the middle were two very tall doors. She flipped on her high beams; the doors were made of metal.

"It looks built to withstand a storm." The upper story consisted of rough-hewn planks and two windows that looked out over the driveway. The steps leading up on the side were stout half logs. She reached behind the seat for her coat and then checked the time.

"Now that I know how to get here, time to find the Whaler's Inn."

But she didn't start the truck. She just sat there, trying to imagine what her new home would be like. Ned's words echoed in the back of her head: *Should I leave your bank account open in case you decide to return?*

When the truck began to bounce from the howling wind, she turned the key, and the old pickup barked to life.

"Get out!"

Joanna peered out the slightly fogged windows for the source of the voice.

"Get out now!"

She turned off the engine and rolled the driver's side window open an inch.

"Hello?"

"Now, get out of now."

Compelled by the bodiless voice, she grabbed her coat and used her full weight to shoulder open the door against the wind. She had just stepped away when it slammed shut. She took a couple of quick steps and turned at the sound of branches cracking. A giant poplar tree came down, crushing the pickup's cab. She ran to the side of the building, to the steps, her hair blowing behind her, pants pressed against her legs, and fluttering like flags. Holding onto a metal rail, she fought her way to the top and the platform in front of the apartment door. She grabbed the doorknob with both hands and wanted to scream in frustration when it wouldn't turn. What was she thinking that it might be unlocked? Descending, she missed the last step and tumbled the remaining foot to the ground.

Soaking wet, bruised, and windblown, Joanna crawled under the steps and curled into a ball. Protected by the side of the building and the steps, she pulled the collar of her coat tight around her neck, closed her eyes, and began to take stock. She had to get out of the storm. When the wind howled around the building, she thought she heard a whine, then something cold and wet pushed against her cheek, making her open her eyes.

"Oh my God, where did you come from?"

The dog was big—maybe a hundred pounds—a rust-colored short hair wearing a vest with bright gold letters spelling out "Rusty—Service Dog." She wrapped an arm around his neck and gave him a hug. "Good boy. Take me to your owner."

As if he understood, Rusty the service dog stepped out into the storm and waited for her to follow.

Joanna staggered out from under the steps, encouraging him. "Good boy, Rusty."

She followed him across the gravel parking area and between two huge red alders to an animal trail. Twenty feet down the trail, Rusty broke away, ran to a fallen tree, and began digging. When she reached his side, she saw an arm sticking out from under a poplar. She felt along the wrist. There was no pulse. Pushing branches aside, she could see that the tree was directly on top of a man, no doubt the owner of the dog.

Joanna grabbed Rusty by the collar. "Come on boy, we've got to get out of this rain. Follow the trail. Show me where it goes."

Rusty reluctantly left his master, and nose to the ground, followed the trail to a stone shelter that was ten feet long by four feet wide. Joanna managed to push the door open, but Rusty just watched. "Come on boy. Rusty, come here." She watched as he curled up next to the door, refusing to enter the shelter. Reluctantly, she pushed the door shut, silencing the noise from the storm, and scooted into a corner.

Surrounded by stones and exhausted from an adrenaline rush that had come and gone several times, she dozed and then fell into a dreamless sleep.

Chapter Three

Joanna woke up to a voice and the wind pushing against her.

"Ma'am, can you stand, Ma'am?"

"Yes, yes."

"My Cruiser is at the museum, is that your truck?"

"Yes."

"Are you hurt? Can you make it down the trail?"

"No, yes just cold and wet."

"I'm Sheriff Jesse Collins, would you happen to be Joanna Bright?"

"Yes. I arrived early-"

"You can explain later," he said and hustled her out of the stone hut.

He wrapped an arm around her waist. "What's the matter with your dog?"

"Huh? What?"

"Looks like he preferred the storm to the shelter."

"Come on Rusty," Joanna said.

Rusty ran up the trail ten feet, then turned and waited.

Collins and Joanna moved like a drunken spider back and forth around deadfalls blocking their way. Rusty ran ahead and then waited for them to catch up.

When they reached the cruiser, Collins opened the rear door and Rusty bounded in. He helped Joanna move against the wind into the passenger side, then ran around and climbed in behind the wheel. "What I'd like to know is how the hell you made it out of the truck to that old stone hut."

She ran a hand over her face as frustration, and helplessness coursed through her, along with the need for a dry, warm place. She ignored his odd question. "Could you find me a room somewhere?"

"We were expecting you for dinner and reserved a room for you at Whalers Inn."

"Oh, wait, my things; they're in the back of the truck."

"I'll send someone to get them. Right now, I want to get you to the Inn and into some warm clothes."

How could this man, the sheriff, be so oblivious to her situation?

"You don't understand. All my clothes are in the back of the truck."

"We'll figure something out. Did you see anybody around the museum, a man about six feet, overweight, with long black hair?"

Joanna wanted to scream. Wasn't it enough that he'd found her huddled in a stone hut, soaked to the skin? "Yeah, I found him under a tree, dead."

"How's that? With all the wind, rain, and trees coming down, you stumbled onto the museum's security guard?"

"Rusty showed me where his master was."

"I see. Rusty."

She couldn't figure out the Sheriff's line of questions. Physically and emotionally exhausted, she gave in to the receding effects of yet another adrenaline rush and fell asleep.

Joanna was jolted awake when the police cruiser stopped. Out the side window, the front of a motel was partly obscured by the porte cochere. Collins opened the door and helped her out of the car, then turned away and marched into the lobby. She opened the rear door and called Rusty to her side. "Hang in there with me boy. I may need a friend."

She took a deep breath, pushed through the double doors, and stepped into the lobby, her shoes wetly slapping on the lobby floor, intent on joining Collins at the front desk. The sheriff turned and held out a keycard.

"This will get you in room three-oh-three. The manager says there's a robe in the bathroom. I'll send someone out to the museum for your things." Without another word, he walked past her. She pivoted, visually following the sheriff as he crossed the lobby and pushed through the double doors. She was surprised when he climbed into the cruiser and drove away.

The hotel manager leaned over the counter and glared at Rusty. "Ma'am. I'm sorry, we don't allow pets in any of the rooms."

She turned back to face the manager. "He's a service dog, and he's with me."

She walked to the elevator with Rusty at her side, then reached down and ruffled his ears, glad that when the doors dinged open, the elevator was empty. With her back against the metal wall, she slid to the floor and fought off a flood of tears that had been building since her ride in the police cruiser. Who were these rude and thoughtless people? Her introduction to Dungeness Bay had been a dead body and a grumpy sheriff all wrapped up in a storm, her only friend a hundred-pound service dog.

When the elevator stopped on the third floor, she pushed herself up. A puddle had formed where she'd been sitting. Soaked to the bone, her clothes felt heavy, like a suit of armor.

Using the keycard, Joanna pushed open the door and beelined it down the hall to the bathroom. A large terrycloth robe hung on the door. She let the shower water heat up as she peeled out of her wet clothes. When she got down to her underwear, it dawned on her that she was being watched.

"Rusty, out," she said and pointed. "You wait out there."

Rusty took the hint and marched down the hall, curling up on an overstuffed chair.

She let the hot water pound on her shoulders as she pondered the voice that had told her to get out of the truck. It couldn't have been the security officer; it looked like he'd been under that tree for a while.

When the water turned cold, she practically leaped from the shower, using three towels to dry off, then padded down the hall in an overly long robe. She headed for the kitchen, where she hoped to find some coffee. Distracted by the smell of wet dog, she backtracked to the living area and called Rusty over. He'd left a wet spot on the cushion where he'd been curled up.

"Come on big guy, I think there are some extra towels in the bathroom."

After fifteen minutes, five wet towels, and a lot of shaking, Rusty was a dry and happy dog.

"Come on, let's find some coffee. Do you drink coffee? Probably not. Let's check out the fridge. Look at this, your namesake." Joanna laughed, "No offense." She took the hot dogs left by the previous occupant out of the refrigerator, set them on a plate for Rusty, and discovered a Keurig coffee maker and some dark French roast pods tucked in a corner, under the cupboards.

Lounging in front of the gas-fueled fireplace with Rusty curled up at her feet and both hands wrapped around her coffee mug, the merit of leaving the Monterey peninsula came to the fore, but her peaceful contemplation was interrupted by a series of loud knocks at the door.

Joanna pulled the robe a little tighter before walking to the door and bringing her eye up to the peephole. The tiny fish-eye lens revealed a man of small stature who was balding, though he still maintained some slightly gray hair. He had sloping shoulders and looked like he had a pillow under his shirt.

"Who is it?"

"Mayor Calvin Ritter. I have your suitcases."

She opened the door and helped the little man bring in her four suitcases.

"Thank you so much. I hope it wasn't a lot of trouble getting them out of the bed of the truck."

"Oh, no trouble for me at all. Alex Jenner ventured out to retrieve them and dropped them off in the lobby a Gulf war Vet, you know—drives the town taxi. I just gave him a call but felt, as mayor, it was my job to bring them up to your room and personally welcome you to Dungeness Bay." He dug into his pocket and produced a set of keys on a ring. "These open the door to your living quarters as well as the museum; they're labeled. Oh, it might help to know that there is a dumbwaiter lift that goes from the back room of the museum to your kitchen."

"Thank you so much."

Calvin walked to the door, then turned. "You should also know that we only reserved this room for one night. You should plan on getting settled tomorrow. I'm sure the storm will have passed by then."

It was getting late when Joanna called the front desk.

"Hello, this is Joanna Bright in three-oh-three. Could you contact the taxi service and arrange to have it pick me up tomorrow morning at nine o'clock?"

"That would be my pleasure, and is there anything else I can do for you?"

"Do you have room service?"

"I'm afraid not. But our restaurant opens at seven-thirty."

"Of course, thank you."

Rusty followed Joanna into the bedroom, watched her climb under the covers, and then curled up at the side of the bed.

Chapter Four

The Whaler's Inn and Restaurant consisted of two buildings separated by a parking lot. The inn had a modern appearance, but the restaurant was a square building with what they called a breakfast bar and a room with rows of booths. Rusty had to remain outside, but Joanna managed to get scraps from the kitchen along with a dented mixing bowl for a dog dish.

She sat in a booth, engaged in mental combat with the drunken monkeys in her mind that wanted to go over and over the events of the day before, but she was determined to put on a good face for the new day. Finished with breakfast, she sipped her coffee, and for just a minute, she let the drunken monkeys win and considered going back to Monterey, then laughed out loud, remembering that a tree had fallen on her truck, dashing that option. No, there was a dog and a taxi waiting for her. She reluctantly drank the last of her coffee and slid out of the booth, left a tip and paid the cashier, then stepped out onto the parking lot.

Rusty was curled up by the door, the mixing bowl empty. He followed her across the lot to the waiting taxi and watched as she peered in the passenger side window. There was no driver. Straightening up, she looked around. The lot was empty. With no apparent options, she strolled back to Whaler's Inn, a little surprised that Rusty was keeping pace.

When she walked into the lobby, the morning manager was talking to a man wearing a black leather jacket, jeans, and tennis shoes. The manager leaned over and gave her a wave.

"This is your taxi driver. Alex Jenner, this is the new curator of the Dungeness Bay Apothecary and Museum, Joanna Bright."

The man appeared to be in his late fifties, with long black hair tied in a ponytail. He took a step forward and extended a hand. "Good to meet you."

"My pleasure. I'd like to thank you for rescuing my suitcases. I wonder if you could help me lug them down to your taxi. I'm moving into the apartment above the museum."

"Not a problem."

Alex walked over to the elevator.

Joanna sighed and thought, *Finally, someone without an attitude—though obviously a man of few words—and good-looking to boot.*

Joanna and Rusty joined him in the elevator, she wasn't sure if she was eager because she wanted to help with the suitcases or to be in the same small space with this man.

He smiled. "Sorry about your truck. It looked like it was totaled."

"I got out just before a tree took out the cab." She decided not to mention the voice that had warned her.

Soon enough, the suitcases were in the trunk and Rusty sat in the back seat with his head resting on Joanna's lap. It was just a fifteen-minute drive to the museum.

Alex pulled up in front of the old Chinese apothecary and Joanna looked around. "What happened to my truck?"

"Sheriff Collins was out here with a tow truck when I arrived to get your things."

"I see."

"Would you like help to take the suitcases up to the apartment?"

"No thanks, I think I can handle it."

"Suit yourself." He pulled a card from his pocket and held it out, "Give me a call if you need a ride back into town."

The insecure part of Joanna wanted to invite this pleasant man up, get to know him, and get a man in her life. It had been six months since K. C. had passed away. Since then, though, she'd made thousands of decisions, including moving north to Dungeness Bay—all without a man. No, she was doing just fine.

"Thank you. Alex, does Dungeness Bay have an auto rental or used car lot or anything like that?"

"Nope. The closest one is in Lincoln City."

Joanna thought about that and said, "Maybe later. I need to get settled first."

He smiled, climbed back in the cab, hung a U-turn, and was gone.

The gravel parking area was dark from the rain. The trees were still dripping, making loud splats as the water struck the leaves that littered the forest floor. Joanna closed her eyes, inhaled the scent of the ocean breeze, and for a moment was back at Stuart's Cove.

When she opened her eyes, for just a heartbeat, she expected K. C. to be at her side.

She looked around at the forest that lined the drive. "The mayor was right; the storm has passed."

She walked up to the tall metal doors of the main building.

"Come on Rusty. Let's find out what I got myself into."

A modern paddle lock looped through a common hole created where the two metal doors came together. The key slipped in easily. She wiggled the padlock loose then pulled it out, hooking it on a belt loop of her jeans until she could find a place to keep it.

Each door had a large handle. She pulled on the right one first, and to her surprise, it moved easily. She pulled it around until it lay flat against the building and did the same with the left-hand door, then stepped back and admired the two twelve-foot-high wooden doors, red with large, foot-high Chinese characters painted in gold.

"We're going to have to find someone who can read these," Joanna said and looked down at Rusty. "Unless you read Chinese."

Rusty sniffed at the base of the doors.

"I didn't think so."

In place of a door handle was a large, key-shaped piece of wood inset into the door on the right. It was nearly a press fit.

"Looks like another key," Joanna observed. "Now if I can just pry it loose."

Unable to get a finger in to force the wooden key out, she pulled the pocketknife she always carried and pried until she thought she'd break the blade.

She could feel the frustration of just one more thing bubbling up and took a calming breath.

"For crying out loud, how the hell do I get the damn thing out?"

In a fit of frustration, she made a fist and lightly punched the wooden key, and watched in fascination as it sprang out, revealing a keyhole.

"Son of a gun," she said, and inserted the key. With some effort, she turned it one hundred and eighty degrees and stepped back as the oversized door slowly moved out of the door jam. She folded it back against the metal door, stepped over the threshold, and covered her mouth and nose. Everything was coated in a blanket of dust. "It smells like the inside of a vacuum cleaner bag."

Rusty was less put off and marched in, leaving dog prints on the dusty floor.

She waved a hand in front of her face. "Rusty, come. I have the feeling my apartment may be in the same condition."

She walked around to the side of the structure and climbed the steps, wondering for the umpteenth time what she'd gotten herself into. The key slipped easily into the lock in the doorknob. The door opened in.

"Thank God, sheets. Hmm, I wonder what the furniture underneath looks like?"

She walked to a sheet that had been draped over a chair, now weighted down with a layer of dust, and gingerly brought the four corners together. Carrying it at arm's length out the door and onto the platform at the top of the steps, she leaned over the rail and let it drop, and then watched as the dust separated from the cloth and formed a cloud that drifted away on a breeze.

The club chair she'd uncovered was upholstered in red leather, as was the couch. The kitchen counter was seasoned wood with a rust-stained porcelain sink.

When Rusty sneezed, Joanna had to laugh. He was covered in dust, his black nose now a dusty brown.

"Two bedrooms. I can't wait to see the bathroom," she said as she walked down the hall and looked down at Rusty. The door was ajar. "Do you want to do the honors?"

As if he understood her, he pushed the door the rest of the way open with his nose.

"Good boy," she said and stepped inside. "It looks like someone brought the bathroom into the 21st century, at least."

There was a window over the shower tub configuration, which was contained by fogged glass sliding doors rather than a plastic curtain. "But why did they stop there?" Joanna wondered. "The floors are plank and the porcelain sink in the kitchen has a built-in washboard circa eighteen eighty." She looked down at Rusty, shrugging. "We may never know."

She walked over to the corner of the living area and gently pulled the dust-laden sheet off a desk. Again, she took it outside and dropped it from the landing at the top of the stairs, then moved back inside with purpose and stopped in front of the desk.

"Would you look at that—a typewriter." She bent down and examined the sheet of paper curled over the roller and picked up half a ream of paper. "This looks like part of a manuscript."

Chapter Five

Joanna set the manuscript down next to the typewriter and walked back into the kitchen and looked over at Rusty, who was sniffing where the wall met the floor just below a large picture on the wall. "Looks like someone left in a hurry. Ugh, I can understand leaving that picture, but who needs a seascape when you live by the ocean?"

With a hand on either side, she lifted up what turned out to be a sheet of Masonite, not a framed canvas.

"Look at that Rusty. It seems you've found the dumbwaiter the mayor mentioned" Joanna inserted four fingers into a slot and lifted, raising a square door that revealed a four-by-four-foot shaft with a rope looped over a pulley that ran straight down.

"Let's go check out the other end of this shaft."

At the bottom of the stairs, she slowed her pace, remembering how she'd missed the last step when she first arrived, and walked around to the front of the building until she was peering into the dusty dinginess of the old apothecary. She reached down and ruffled the hair between Rusty's ears and considered the work that would have to go into cleaning up what the city considered a museum.

"Oh Rusty, what have I gotten myself into?" Joanna paused, checking her watch. "Twelve thirty? No wonder I'm hungry. We can investigate the lift later. Do you suppose there's a phone in here somewhere?"

Rather than venture in, Joanna walked around the entire building, Rusty at her side. Not finding any wires, she concluded that there was, in fact, no phone. She slipped her cell phone out of her hip pocket, looking at it in dismay. "No service." She looked down at Rusty. "How do you feel about a walk into town?"

She looked over at the suitcases waiting to be moved upstairs, tipped one over, unzipped the top, and pulled out a long-sleeved sweater. As an afterthought, she moved all four suitcases just inside the apothecary and smiled at Rusty, who was taking it all in. "Just in case it rains."

She swung the large wooden doors shut and turned at the sound of a motorcycle. "Looks like we've got company, Rusty. Maybe we won't have to walk to town after all."

The motorcycle, which had a sidecar, approached, and for a moment, Joanna wondered if she should be looking for a quick exit. But with Rusty at her side, she sensed that he would protect her. The rider pulled up about ten feet away, turned off the engine, and dismounted. She gave a nervous laugh when Alex took off his helmet.

"Hey," he greeted, indicating his bike with a wave of his hand. "It's a Ural."

She laughed again. "Sorry, but that just sounds too close to urinal."

"That's Ural, not urinal. It's Russian."

"It's just that since I've arrived in Dungeness Bay, my truck's been crushed, and I was warned away by a disembodied voice. I've found a dead body, but I've also made a friend." Joanna knelt down and pulled Rusty into a hug. "And now the urin—I mean, the Ural. What brings you back?"

Alex walked around to the back of the sidecar and opened the trunk. "I'm sorry to hear all that. I remembered that you'd have no phone or cell service and thought you might be hungry, so I brought lunch." He held up a bag. "I hope you like Chinese. I thought it would be appropriate seeing where you're going to be working."

"My apartment is a dusty mess, but there is a writer's desk I just cleared off."

He took out a six-pack of beer, then dropped his leather jacket and helmet into the trunk of the sidecar and elbowed the lid shut. "Fine by me."

Joanna wondered what she was doing inviting a complete stranger up to her apartment but was a little less apprehensive with Rusty at her heel.

Alex set the bag of Chinese food and the six pack at the end of the desk and looked at the typewriter. "This must have belonged to Thayer Spelling. She came up here to write a story about Dungeness Bay. She hadn't been in town for a while. When the sheriff and I came up to check on her, she was gone."

Joanna slid the typewriter to the far end of the long desk. "You know what, I don't have any plates or silverware."

"Not to worry; look here," Alex said, pulling the wire handles out of the food containers and pushing the sides down flat. He reached back into the bag and pulled out two sets of chopsticks. "Viola."

"Perfect," Joanna said, and the two of them chowed down. "Where'd you learn to use chopsticks like that?"

"I spent some time in San Francisco's Chinatown."

"What can you tell me about the museum?"

"Not much, except that they can't keep the help."

"That might explain all the dust. How long ago was Thayer Spelling here?"

"I don't know—a few months, maybe. She was the last in a long line of tenants. The city was going to tear the place down, but the mayor got a group together and talked the city council into trying one more time to get an occupant." He caught Joanna's eye. "That would be you."

"Any idea what drove the others off?"

"Ghosts. At least, that's what the ones who bothered to contact the sheriff before taking off said."

Joanna finished her beer and set the bottle on the floor. "So, what brought you to Dungeness Bay, and what keeps you here?"

"The first Gulf War left me with post-traumatic stress disorder, which brought me here. The population is why I stay."

"I understand PTSD, but not the part about the population."

Alex shrugged. "It's a small town. I cleaned up my car and wrote 'taxi' on the side to earn a living—well, with the help of a pension from Uncle Sam and medical Social Security. Everybody knows everybody, but for the most part, they leave each other alone, and that includes me."

"Got it. I'm glad you showed up. It would have been a long walk to town."

"You're just outside cell service here, and I have to admit, my coming back had to do with a personal agenda."

Joanna felt a little uneasy by that. She looked around for Rusty, who was asleep at her feet under the desk.

"And what would that be?"

Alex dropped the uneaten Chinese food and the cartons in the bag. "You can keep the beer. Let's go back outside and I'll lay it out for you. You know, what I'm thinking could be a win for both of us."

Joanna followed Alex downstairs with no small amount of trepidation as he walked over to the sidecar. He opened the trunk, pulled out his jacket and helmet, and dropped the bag in before saying, "See, you've got a transportation problem, and I have a solution."

She came over and sat on the nose of the sidecar. "You found a car for me?"

"Not exactly," Alex said and smiled sheepishly. "I found this Ural for you."

Chapter Six

Joanna hopped off the sidecar. "What? Are you joking? I can't ride a motorcycle."

"Now hear me out."

She gave Rusty, who had jumped into the sidecar, a dirty look and folded her arms.

Alex continued, "Forty-five miles to the gallon. The trunk could hold groceries and, as you can see, the sidecar can carry your friend."

"I have no idea how to drive this thing."

"You ever ride a tricycle?"

"Of course."

"It turns the same way, no leaning like a motorcycle, and as you can see three wheels."

"No, this is ridiculous," Joanna protested.

"Okay then, hop in the sidecar with your friend and I'll take you into town so you can buy some silverware, plates, and the like."

"I'm not getting into that sidecar. Wait a minute. You planned this, didn't you?"

"It's true that I do have to get back to my taxi business, but that means that I would be leaving you here with no food or phone. Come on; what can it hurt?"

"Okay, fine. You've got me over a barrel. I'll ride into town. Wait, no, no. How will I get back?"

"I'll tell you what. You let me teach you how to drive the Ural and I'll find you a car as soon as I can."

Joanna turned in a circle and wanted to scream. "That doesn't make any sense."

"It makes total sense. I can't be hauling you back and forth. There are no cars for sale in Dungeness Bay, and as much as I'd like to take you north to Lincoln City to buy a car, I won't be free to do that until next week. I do understand your situation and have brought you the solution. All you have to do is demonstrate some intestinal fortitude."

Joanna bristled. "Let me tell you something about intestinal fortitude. My husband of thirty years died six months ago. I've sold my physical therapy practice and everything I own and moved out of the only home I've known since I was twenty-two, which includes leaving the Monterey Peninsula to come here, of all places."

Alex walked around to the front of the sidecar and wrapped an arm around her shoulder. "You're right. Make a list, and I'll come back tomorrow with everything you need."

She stepped back, removing herself from his arm and letting out a sigh. "How hard is it really, you know, to learn to ride this thing?"

Alex smiled and handed her the key. "If you're game, I can have you comfortable and turning circles in half an hour."

"You're on. You've got exactly half an hour."

"Scoot over boy," Alex said to Rusty as he stepped into the sidecar. "Climb on, put in the key, and press the black button by the right-hand grip."

Joanna followed his directions, and with a slight growl, the engine started. "How do I make it go?"

"Not so fast. The left grip is your clutch. Squeeze it a couple of times. The one on the right is your front brake. Do the same thing; squeeze it a couple of times. You shift first, second, and third with your left toe, but not yet. Your right foot pushes the pedal that puts on the rear brake.

"Now what I want you to do is press down with your right foot when I tell you to. First, pull in the clutch." He watched Joanna squeeze the lever. "Good. Now push down into first gear with your left foot. Great. Notice that you're not going anywhere. Now squeeze the right lever for the front brake and hold it tight, and slowly release the left lever, the clutch."

In twenty minutes, Joanna was turning circles in the gravel

parking area, then figure eights and quick stops, and reversing. She turned the engine off and pulled out the key.

"What's the problem?"

"Your half hour is up."

Alex chuckled and climbed out of the sidecar. "What do you think?"

"I'm tense as hell, and you're as good as your word."

"Great, now for your test."

"What?" Joanna looked at him with trepidation.

"It's two o'clock. I need to get back to town. I want you to drive the length of the driveway. Then, we'll switch places and I'll take us through town."

Again, Alex was as good as his word, and after some shopping, Joanna watched him walk away without a backward glance. "Guess we're on our own, big guy," she said to Rusty. "You'd better hang on."

Upon her return, Joanna parked the Ural sidecar rig in front of the apothecary just after five o'clock, the trunk filled with dishes and produce. Rusty hopped out, gave a shake, and watched her dismount.

"What do you think, fella?" she asked. She held her hand out and watched it shake. "Wow, I'm a little tense from that drive. Let's go check out that dumbwaiter." She opened the big wooden door and pushed one of the suitcases to one side, staring at the floor and the words in the dust that read *Get Out.*

"Great. Next time I'll lock the door."

She dragged her foot over the message as she crossed the main room and pushed the door open to the storage area. "Okay, another seascape." She removed the Masonite, exposing the door of the lift. But this time, when she slid the door up, the four-by-four car was exposed.

"Great; let's load in the groceries."

She filled the dumbwaiter car in three trips, then ran up the stairs, where hand over hand, she pulled on the rope and brought the car up, then pulled down the lever that locked the rope against the pulley.

"This is great. What do you think, Rusty?" He wasn't at her side, so she looked around and found him curled up under the desk. "Well, you're a big help."

Chapter Seven

Cleaning the apartment was a slow process. All the cupboards had to be cleaned first and the fridge had to be wiped down. When Joanna finished putting everything away, she sat down at the desk with one of the beers Alex had left and was beginning to relax when the lever that locked the rope to the pulley let go and the lift plummeted the twenty-five feet to the apothecary below and made a deep thump like a timpani drum.

Rusty came out from underneath the desk and stuck close to Joanna's side as she descended the steps, came around to the front of the building and opened one of the big wooden doors.

She walked past the racks of herbs into the back storage room, where she stared at the dumbwaiter car, which remained undamaged. "What do you think, boy? Want to take the little car back up?" But when she turned to address Rusty, he was ten paces back with his hackles standing up and a low growl coming from his throat.

"That's okay, boy," she said. "Nothing's broken. Let's get upstairs and finish cleaning."

By nine o'clock, Joanna called it quits. She polished off the last bottle of beer and decided to check out the partial manuscript she'd found by the typewriter. When Rusty came out from under the desk and walked to the door, she put the manuscript down, and, moments later, heard tires on the gravel. She opened the door and walked out onto the platform, pleased that Rusty stayed at her side. Joanna saw the word Taxi on the side of the stopped car.

She looked at Rusty. "Hey boy, you think Alex wants his Ural back?"

In response, Rusty wagged his tail.

"I hope I'm not coming by too late?" Alex asked as he stepped out of his car.

"Not at all. What's up?" she yelled down.

"I'm going to be out of town for a couple of days and thought I'd drop off my shop vacuum. I'll just leave it here by the doors."

He lugged the big vacuum out of the trunk of his car.

"Thank you."

"No problem. Have a good night and happy cleaning."

Joanna watched him drive off and, for a moment, wished she'd invited him up on some pretense.

Tired, she climbed under the new sheets on her new mattress and watched as Rusty settled at the foot of her bed. She fell into a deep sleep until the sound of Rusty's nails clicking on the plank floor woke her up.

She sat up and tapped the side of the bed with her hand; Rusty came over and licked her fingers. "That's okay boy, probably just critters in the walls." He circled twice, then lay down by the side of the bed.

Joanna surprised herself by getting up at sunrise. She'd never been an early riser but felt rested, and Rusty was waiting by the door. She changed from pj's to jeans and a sweatshirt.

"Come on, let's get some coffee and check out the beach."

While the coffee was brewing, she filled a dish with kibble and set it out on the landing at the top of the steps, then leaned on the rail and listened to the breeze rustle the leaves of the poplar trees.

The Kam Wah apothecary sat on a high bluff above the beach. While Rusty played tag with the ebb and flow of the tide, Joanna took off her tennis shoes, rolled up her jeans, and waded through several tide pools, but stopped, she could just make out the sound of tires crunching on the gravel above the roar of the ocean.

"Rusty, I think we've got company," she yelled and ran toward the path that led up the bluff and would take her to the side of the apothecary. As soon as she began to run, Rusty moved to be at her side, then he ran up the trail, wagging his tail, waiting for her to catch up.

But when Joanna got to the top of the bluff, the parking area was empty. She walked around to the front of the building and saw a slip of paper rolled up and stuck under the handle of the shop vac. She pulled it out, thinking that it was a note from Alex, and then wadded it up after reading the words *get out.*

"Looks like we did have company." Joanna looked at Rusty, concerned.

Rusty looked around, then followed her up the steps to her apartment, but she didn't enter. Instead, she sat on the wooden platform, Rusty lying next to her.

"You know, I think someone doesn't want us to stick around."

She got up, walked into the apartment, leaving the door open, and tried to shake a feeling of melancholy that maybe, just maybe, Ned was right, and she should move back to the Monterey Peninsula. She shook off her sense of doubt and decided on a hearty breakfast instead. She probably just needed some protein. Three eggs and as many pieces of bacon later, she was feeling optimistic about her decision to come to Dungeness Bay.

The shop vacuum worked wonders on the floor but was too clumsy for the nooks between bottles and boxes of herbs. What Joanna really needed was a hand vac. She looked down at Rusty. "I think we'll break for lunch."

Walking around the far side of the building where she'd parked the Ural, she found another note on the seat of the sidecar. *Leave.* For the first time, she wished Alex would get back early.

The Ural started easily. She was in second gear and accelerating up the slight incline of the driveway when Dungeness Bay's main drag came into sight. She tapped the right peddle for the rear bake to no effect. She squeezed the lever for the front disc brake, but again, nothing. Downshifting to cut her speed, she killed the engine and brought the sidecar rig to an abrupt stop, cranked on the emergency brake, and sat for a minute, wondering if she had somehow done something wrong. Then she remembered the note.

Joanna dismounted and looked under the motorcycle until she found the brake line and the slice that was still leaking fluid. She lifted the trunk lid, pulled out a leash for Rusty, and began the walk into town. She needed an alarm system and a gun. No one was going to scare her into leaving Dungeness Bay.

Chapter Eight

Joanna stood on the top rung of a rickety extension ladder she had found in the back room of the apothecary. She put a contact plate for the alarm on the top of the big wooden door and matched it with one on the door jam. At each corner of the front of the building, she placed a motion-sensitive light. At the base of the two poplar trees that marked the edge of the parking area, she placed a motion sensor that would trigger the camera. It was low so she could get a good shot of a license plate if a car were to approach.

Dinner—stir-fried vegetables—took place out on the landing. She was basking in her handiwork when she heard a car coming up the gravel drive, relieved when she recognized Alex's taxi. He bolted out and ran up the steps, upsetting Rusty in the process.

"I saw the Ural at the top of the drive. Is everything all right?"

Joanna fought the urge to hug him, if for nothing more than his concern. The urge quickly passed, and she set her plate on the rail instead.

"Someone left a couple notes telling me to get out, then they cut the brake line on the Ural. But I'm ready for them."

"How so?"

"Motion sensor lights, and this," she said pulling a Glock 19 from the holster in the middle of her back.

"Oh, shit. Put that away, and let's go inside and talk about this."

"I wasn't expecting you to come around for another couple of days."

"My schedule changed. Now talk to me."

"Have you eaten? I've got some extra stir fry."

"I grabbed dinner in town, but I'd take a beer. Now tell me about your day."

Joanna sighed as she motioned for Alex to follow her inside. "It started last night. Rusty was up, and I figured it was critters—you know, raccoons or something. Then this morning, we went for a walk on the beach. I'm sure I heard a car on the drive, but when I got up here, all I found was a note on your shop vacuum and one on the Ural, both telling me to get out. I was lucky the brakes failed before I blended with traffic."

"The alarm and lights are smart, but not the gun."

"I know, but I needed something. The notes are one thing but cutting my brake line takes the threat to the next level."

Joanna settled on the couch. Alex pulled a club chair around to face her.

"There's nothing we can do tonight. Just stay vigilant."

"What's going on, Alex? Why does someone want me to leave? And don't tell me I've got ghosts here."

He took a long swig of his beer before replying. "There's supposed to be gold somewhere on the premises. The story has been around as long as this apothecary."

"You mean here in this building, or buried gold somewhere on the grounds?" Joanna asked, sitting forward. "Pirate gold?"

"No, nothing like that. Kam Wah and his partner, Lung On, helped ailing and sick miners who paid in gold from their mines. The problem was, the exclusion act of 1882 didn't allow the Chinese to own or operate a business. If either of the partners had attempted to cash in the gold, it would have revealed that they were operating a business and they probably would have been driven out of town on a rail."

"Shit."

"Yeah. During the 1918 flu epidemic, their practice kept the town folk healthy as well as the mass of aging miners. Anyway, the story is that they hid the gold somewhere in the apothecary."

"Right, and whoever wrote me those notes is probably the same person who scared away Thayer Spelling."

"Probably, but they must think they know where the gold is. Cutting your brake line is the first violent act, at least that I know of."

Joanna pulled the gun from its holster from the middle of her back and leaned into the couch. "This may be a bad idea," she said, "but I'll sleep better because of it."

Alex stood and added, "Just don't shoot Rusty."

Joanna let out a chuckle and got up. "Thanks for coming by," she said, walking over to give him a hug. "See you tomorrow?"

Alex smiled. "Yeah, I'll help you clean and look for hidden gold."

She walked him out onto the landing and, for just a moment, felt like a schoolgirl at the end of a date waiting for a kiss. Joanna let the feeling go and watched him descend the stairs, climb in the taxi, and drive off.

With a sigh, she sat down and gave Rusty a hug. "Come on, let's go inside and be vigilant."

Rusty settled under the desk—a favorite spot of his, Joanna noticed—when she picked up the manuscript and slumped into the club chair. But it wasn't the opening hook or even the middle chapters that caught her interest. It was the last chapter: the way it mentioned the miners and the gold they paid with and the locals who paid in cash or checks. The more she read over that chapter and the way it ended, teasing the reader into reading the next chapter and the rest of the manuscript to find out what happened to the gold, cash, and checks, the more intrigued she became. Joanna wished she had the rest of the manuscript.

Finally, blurry-eyed and under the influence of three beers, Joanna shuffled around the living room, collecting empty beer bottles and dropping them into a box for recycling in the kitchen. She headed for the little hall that led to the two bedrooms and the bathroom, then abruptly turned and stumbled back into the living room, where she retrieved her gun.

"Come on, time for bed," she said to Rusty.

Rusty had just curled up at the foot of the bed when a loud moan came up through the floorboards. Rusty was instantly on his feet, his head swiveling from the door to Joanna, who was sitting on the side of the bed fingering her Glock 19.

Chapter Nine

She patted the side of the bed until Rusty came over. "Lay down," she ordered, then grabbed three pillows and stacked them at the foot of the bed. She lay down facing the door, gun resting on the top pillow.

"If someone comes through the door, it will be the last thing they do," Joanna said, and slowly fell asleep. She spiraled up from a deep sleep, not fully awake but not fully conscious, either. She felt the gun against her hand and grasped it, taking aim at the middle of the door and continuing to doze.

Outside, Alex stood in front of his taxi with his hands on his hips, staring at the landing and the apartment door. Joanna hadn't responded to the sound of him driving up by coming out. Bells and whistles went off in his mind, and he ran up the stairs and knocked once, only to have the door swing open. With all the stealth he could muster, he crossed the floor, then laughed, feeling silly that he wasn't just calling out to her.

Joanna blinked awake at the sound of Rusty's growl. She shook her head, trying to clear the fog, then heard footfalls on the planks in the living room. Rusty was at the door, still growling. She tapped the side of the bed until he came over, then sagged into the bed. She sighted the gun on the middle of the door, finger on the trigger.

Alex stopped in his tracks. The words *get out* were written in what looked like blood on the hall wall. He shook his head and cursed under his breath.

That was all it took. Joanna could just make out someone in her apartment whispering. Were there two intruders? She took a deep, calming breath and pulled the trigger.

The sound of the shot occurred seconds before the door splintered. Alex dropped to the floor, shouting, "Joanna! Joanna, it's Alex. Everything is all right. Put the gun down." He crept to the door on his hands and knees and grabbed the doorknob. "I'm going to open the door."

When he stood and opened the door, he saw Rusty blocking his way growling, showing his teeth.

"What the hell is going on? Are you all right? Your front door was open, and someone wrote another note on your wall."

Joanna rolled to the side of the bed. "About ten or eleven, someone down in the apothecary moaned so loud that it came up through the floorboards. Honestly, I'm about done with all this ghost stuff. What are you doing here so early anyway?"

"I was concerned. When you didn't respond to the sound of me driving up, I came upstairs. Your door wasn't latched, so I wasn't sure what to expect."

Joanna pinched the bridge of her nose. "Okay. First things first. Get out of here and let me get dressed."

"How about I fix breakfast?" Alex offered.

"Perfect. By the way, I found something in the last chapter of the manuscript I'd like to show you—maybe over eggs and hash browns?"

"I'll see what I can do."

Joanna was pleased when she came into the kitchen. Alex had not only made breakfast but had also set the table and placed the manuscript in the middle.

"Have a seat," Alex said.

He slid the bacon eggs and hash browns from pan to plate, and set it in front of her. "What did you find in the manuscript?"

"Read the last chapter and give me your impression," she said and forked into the eggs. "Hey, where's Rusty?"

Alex looked up from the manuscript. "I put some kibble out on the landing."

"Thank you for that. He's been quite the companion."

After breakfast, he washed and she dried, and they decided to tackle the apothecary and dig into the manuscript around dinner.

Joanna began cleaning bottles and shelves nearest the door, which was virtually the only source of light. Alex was going around replacing light bulbs.

"I hope all these new bulbs aren't more than the old circuits can bear. I'm going up onto the loft."

"Watch yourself on that ladder," Joanna cautioned. "It looks pretty rickety."

She stopped her cleaning and watched Alex climb the ladder. She was about to return to the shelf she'd been working on when he called down to her.

"We've got footprints in the dust. Have you been up here?"

"No, I was saving the loft for last."

Alex stepped to the edge of the loft then turned and leaned on the rail. He was saying something when the rail gave way and he somersaulted over the edge and down the fifteen feet to the plank floor below, landing on his back. Joanna ran to his side, but he was unconscious. There was no blood, but she was afraid to move him, and decided to make a run into town in his taxi.

When she slid behind the wheel, she saw that the key was in the ignition. Instead of driving into town as she had planned, Joanna grabbed the mic for the two-way and was greeted by a man who identified himself as a ham radio operator. He said he'd send an ambulance down from Lincoln City, but it would take about half an hour.

She ran back inside the apothecary and kneeled over Alex who was still unconscious.

The mayor's voice made Joanna turn toward the door. "Ms. Bright, are you in there?"

"Yes, back here. Alex fell from the loft and he's unconscious. An ambulance is on the way."

The mayor crossed the floor and looked over her shoulder. "My lord. What happened?"

"I'm not sure, but I think he was leaning on the rail and it couldn't support his weight."

The mayor seemed at a loss for words. "Is there anything I can do?"

"I think you should contact the sheriff."

"Certainly. Oh wait, I think he's at the morgue in Lincoln City. I'll go to the police office and see if dispatch can reach him."

Joanna watched the mayor leave, wondering why he had stopped by. When she turned back around, Alex opened his eyes. She placed a hand on his chest.

"You've taken a terrible fall, and an ambulance is on the way. You shouldn't try to move."

His lips moved but the words came out in a whisper. "What?" she said, and leaned down close, then straightened up. Alex had closed his eyes.

"Cell phone." Joanna frowned. "Why would you mention your cell phone unless there's something on it that you want me to see?"

As Joanna puzzled over what Alex had said, the ambulance finally arrived, followed by the sheriff.

"Ms. Bright, could I have a word?"

She nodded, stood, and stepped next to the sheriff. Together, they watched as Alex was carried on a stretcher to the ambulance.

"Ma'am, how well do you know Alex?"

"He's been a good friend since I've arrived at Dungeness Bay. Why?"

"Alex Jenner has become a person of interest in a local homicide. I'd appreciate it if you'd come down to the police station to answer a few questions."

Chapter Ten

The Dungeness Bay police department was a small brick structure built in 1915 to house the fire department. It was the first structure in the young community to have electricity. The fire chief lived upstairs, and the garage was just large enough for the water wagon. The building was abandoned when water wagons were replaced with pumper trucks. The new fire department was constructed to accommodate the five-man police department but burned to the ground in 1997.

With massive budget cuts raging through most Oregon Counties, the city council laid off the entire fire and police department, pulled former Sheriff Jesse Collins out of retirement, and swore in a former security guard, Chuck Cowdrey, from a defunct strip mall who'd inherited a beach bungalow in town, as a junior deputy slash dispatcher. They had the old brick firehouse rewired and with no fire department christened it the Dungeness Bay Police Department in bold black letters against a white background and hung the sign over the big front door.

Sheriff Collins pulled his cruiser into the oversized garage, got out, walked around, and held the door to the main building for Joanna, who was still trying to get her head around the idea that Alex was a person of interest in a homicide.

Collins walked her into a back room, the largest space on the main floor except for the garage.

"Please take a seat. I'm going to call in my deputy, who will witness and record your response to my questions."

"Is that really necessary?"

"I could ask Louis Johnson, owner of the Book Nook, to sit in if you'd prefer a woman to be present instead of my deputy."

"I'm fine with your deputy."

Collins walked around the small desk and out of the office.

When he returned, he was followed by a rather rotund, youngish officer, who took a seat in the corner.

"Joanna Bright, this is Deputy Chuck Cowdrey."

When she looked over, Cowdrey gave a smile and a nod.

"Start the recorder, Chuck. Joanna Bright, how long have you been in Dungeness Bay?"

"Four days."

"When did you first meet Alex Jenner?"

"The day after I arrived."

"What were the circumstances of that meeting?"

"I was staying at the Whaler's Inn, and he brought down my suitcases and loaded them into his taxi." Joanna paused. "Honestly, is this necessary? I'm afraid I can't answer any more questions without knowing what Alex is being accused of."

"Ma'am, my line of questions are based on plausible deniability. That is to say, if you have inadvertently, though your association with Mister Jenner, been involved in a criminal act, you can claim no knowledge of the crime."

"What exactly are you accusing Alex of doing?"

"If I reveal this to you, you may no longer claim ignorance."

"Ignorance of what?"

"Ignorance of the murder of Gus Hasselbacker."

"Who?"

"The body you found the day you arrived in Dungeness Bay."

"This is insane. It was his service dog, Rusty, that led me to his body. He was killed when a tree fell on him."

"I just came from a meeting with the medical examiner at Lincoln City's morgue, where Gus's body was taken. He said the autopsy showed that Gus was already dead when the tree fell on him and that he had been struck on the head with his own cane, creating enough blunt force trauma to kill him."

"When you said you'd send someone out for my things, Gus was already dead," Joanna said.

Collins looked at Chuck and drew his hand across his throat. "Stop recording. Ma'am, I had the unpleasant task of calling Gus's brother, his only next of kin, and telling him that Gus had been killed and that his death was under investigation, and that any time, at least in the state of Oregon, when someone dies alone, an autopsy is required. Ms. Bright, he about talked my ear off. Turns out that Alex and Gus had served in the same unit in the first Gulf War, and that despite a bullet to the knee taken during a firefight, Gus had carried a wounded Alex Jenner to safety.

"I did a little investigating and discovered that after discharge, Gus moved to Dungeness Bay, but Alex moved onto the street. He has a police record—drunk and disorderly, served sixty days in a San Jose jail. Then his father died, and he ended up in Four South at Agnew State Mental Hospital for a month. When he got out, he shacked up with a woman, the sister of Michael Lars, a drug kingpin. Then he just dropped out of sight. But of all things strange, the guy inherits just under a million bucks from one of his father's investments."

"Alex told me he suffered from PTSD," Joanna responded. "He said he'd had a rough time living in the city and moved to Dungeness Bay to get away from the masses."

"Do you know what? I think you're right. But when he got here, he ran into Gus, who somehow knew of the inheritance and of Alex's police record. You see, Alex had a parole officer and was restricted from leaving the state, and Oregon must have looked like a safe place. If Gus turned him in, Alex would be taken back to California, where he would serve time. I believe Gus was blackmailing him. I have a witness in good standing who says he saw Alex giving money to Gus on several occasions. Do you know what it takes to convict someone of murder? Means, motive, and opportunity. Alex certainly had a motive, which would be getting out from underneath the blackmailer. Means—well, that would have been Gus's own cane—and the storm was the perfect opportunity."

Chapter Eleven

Sheriff Collins continued, "I think they were meeting for the final payoff and Gus got greedy and demanded more. In a rage, Alex snatched the cane from an ailing Gus Hasselbacker and struck him on the head, and left him for dead. It was only by coincidence that the tree fell on him."

Joanna stood. "I'm hearing a lot of 'I believe this, and I think that.' Do you know what I think? I think you're grasping at straws because you don't know who really killed Gus. Right now, Alex is in a coma in the Lincoln City hospital, unable to defend himself. Until he can, I'm afraid I'll hold my judgment," Joanna said, taking a calming breath. "Accusing a man who can't speak for himself is despicable. I'd like to go back to my apartment now."

Collins slowly stood. "Chuck, take Ms. Bright back to the apothecary. Oh, and Ms. Bright, you can bet I'll be at Alex's bedside the moment he wakes up."

Joanna followed the deputy back into the garage and then out to the front parking area. He held the door of his American Motors Gremlin open.

"The car's kind of a mess," Cowdrey said by way of apology.

"You don't drive a cruiser?"

"Budget cuts and all, you know." Cowdrey eyed Joanna. "Listen, I just want you to know that I agree with what you said back there. I had a friend who came back from the first Gulf War with PTSD. It took a couple years for him to get it together."

"Thank you."

They rode in silence down the main drag until he took the turnoff for the apothecary. When they arrived, Cowdrey said, "I know you don't have a phone that works. I could come back and check on you if you'd like."

"I'll be okay, but thanks for the offer."

Cowdrey nodded. "You have a good rest of your day."

Joanna opened the big doors of the apothecary and watched Rusty bound out. She walked around to the side of the building, relieved that the Ural was intact, grateful that Alex was able to replace the brake line. She was hungry, and angry at the sheriff, and at the same time wondering if Alex really was connected to the death of Gus Hasselbacker.

When she unlocked her apartment door she paused, then turned and watched Rusty run up the steps. She pushed the door open, but he didn't enter until she did.

"Well, aren't you polite?"

Once inside, he curled up under the desk. Joanna went straight to the closet and pulled out the only suitcase she hadn't unpacked and lugged it up on the bed.

She unzipped the side and began pulling out books until she came across a wire-bound volume, the word *Journal* printed in bold block letters on the front.

"There you are."

She hadn't journaled since she arrived in Dungeness Bay.

Back in the living room, Joanna settled into the club chair. She flipped to a blank page and labeled the top with the date, day, and time. Then began as she always did.

Dear Journal,

Today I learned that a man I consider my friend, Alex Jenner, has a troubled past. It seems my only real friend is a service dog that somehow found me on the stormy day I arrived. I had no idea when I responded to the ad for a museum tour guide and caretaker that I was going to be so isolated. No phone and no cell service. Maybe I shouldn't have left the peninsula.

No. This is the change I needed—a fresh start after caring for K. C. all those months. Plus, there were the tourists and all that traffic. No. This is my chance to, as Alex said, show some intestinal fortitude. After all, I did learn to drive a Russian motorcycle with a sidecar. K. C. would be so proud of me. If only he were here now.

Joanna paused in her journaling and decided it was time to continue her lifelong routine. She got up and placed the pen and journal on the desk. Rusty followed her down the steps but stopped as she stepped off the last step. He watched as she walked to the middle of the graveled parking area.

She turned to face north, placed her feet shoulder-width apart, and began her tai chi. Then she stopped and took some calming breaths to clear the drunken monkeys from her mind—wu wei, the state of no-mind. She began again and completed her various exercises: ball rolling, grasping bird's tail, wave hands like clouds. Finished with the Yang style's short 52 forms, she began her chi kung. Twenty minutes later, she knew what she would do and looked over at Rusty.

"I've been teaching tai chi for thirty years. What better way to get acquainted with the community? I think I'm going to like it here."

Back in the apartment, she puttered around. Everywhere she looked, there was something, some shelf, that still needed to be dusted or scrubbed, Then there was that horrid ottoman, but she'd deal with that later.

She went to the desk and made up a flyer, then looked at her watch. It was twelve o'clock. Lincoln City was only twenty minutes away, a straight run north up Highway 101. They'd have a print shop where she could make copies of her flyer for her tai chi class, and she could visit Alex. This would be the longest trip on the Ural. She looked at Rusty.

"What do think? Are you up for a trip?"

She wasn't sure but thought Rusty was smiling.

She left Dungeness Bay behind and was pleased with the Ural until she was hit with the first gust of wind and was nearly blown off the road.

Chapter Twelve

At sixty miles an hour, the motorcycle was nearly flat out. Joanna could feel the engine working, then she remembered to check her mirrors and immediately pulled over to let a row of cars pass. Fifteen minutes later, with a gap in traffic, she accelerated back onto the road and pushed the Russian motorcycle to its maximum of sixty-eight miles an hour. As soon as she entered Lincoln City, she pulled into the first gas station, parked, stretched, put Rusty on a leash, and walked him out to a little patch of grass.

The Lincoln City hospital was really a clinic. It had an ER and several doctors on staff. Alex was in the special intensive care center located at the back of the facility. Joanna entered through the front and asked for the room of Alex Jenner, surprised when the nurse told her that the more people who visited him, the sooner he would come out of his coma. For a heart-stopping moment, she wondered if Sheriff Collins was visiting.

When she entered the room, two men were standing on both sides of the bed. One turned to face her.

"Hi there, do you know Alex?" The man said.

"Yes, he helped me out when I moved to Dungeness Bay,"

He took a step in her direction and extended a hand. "William Snow. This is John."

She shook his hand and nodded at John. "How did you know him?"

"We served with him in the first Gulf War, the one hundred and first airborne. We got word that a fellow veteran was in a coma and was going to be transferred to the San Francisco VA. When I checked into the ID, I saw that it was Alex. So, we had to come up. We were already up in Dungeness Bay; we heard that Gus Hasselbacker was killed in a storm."

Joanna relaxed and walked to the foot of the bed. "You guys knew Gus?"

"Oh yeah, he was one of us. Took a bullet and fell on hard times."

She walked over to the side of the bed and took Alex's hand. "Did you talk to the sheriff in Dungeness Bay?"

"No, we came up here when we heard Gus was in the morgue."

"The sheriff thinks that Gus was blackmailing Alex and that Alex killed him," Joanna said.

"What?"

John turned on Joanna so fast she took a step back.

"Sheriff's full of it," Snow said. "Alex came to Dungeness Bay because he heard Gus was hitting the skids, really having a hard time. Gus pulled Alex out of a firefight, and Alex never forgot."

"What about his PTSD?"

"You know, a Gulf War vet had three days after discharge to file, and back in the day, no one called it PTSD. We all dealt with it in different ways."

Joanna let out a deep breath. "I have a big favor to ask."

John looked across the bed at her. "Yeah, what?"

"The Dungeness Bay sheriff is about to throw Alex under the bus. Go talk to him. His name's Jesse Collins. Tell him what you just told me."

"Problem is," Snow said, "Alex is in the wrong state for the right reason, but your sheriff won't care and will send him back to California, where he'll serve time for breaking parole. And even if he doesn't, if Alex stays in a coma, he'll still end up in California. That's where he'll wake up, and when he does, he'll serve time."

"Tell you what, you talk to the sheriff, and I'll bring in a California attorney," Joanna said.

At this, John and Snow exchanged looks. John walked around to Joanna's side of the bed and stuck out his hand. "Deal. We'll straighten out the sheriff."

"I'll take care of keeping Alex in Oregon. Right now, I've got to get back to Dungeness Bay."

"We're going to hang out here for a bit," John said, smiling for the first time.

Joanna figured she'd get a hold of Ned, who would know how to keep Alex in Oregon, but she'd need access to a landline to make the call.

When she rolled into town and passed the police department, she remembered Deputy Cowdrey. She turned around and parked in front of the old brick building, breathed a sigh of relief at the sight of the empty garage, and entered the little lobby where the deputy was manning dispatch.

"Oh, hey Joanna, how are you doing?" Cowdery asked.

"Fine, but I've got a favor to ask."

"Shoot."

"Do you live in town?"

"Sure do. I inherited one of the beach bungalows. Why?"

"I need access to a landline."

"Oh yeah, that's right, you don't have any cell service or even a landline out there. No problem; today's my half day. You could drop by a little after two o'clock."

"I don't know where the bungalows are, and you need to know that I'll be calling my attorney in California about Alex." Joanna figured honesty was the best policy.

"Just take a right at the light onto Ocean Avenue and follow it. I'm the last bungalow on the right. Just make your call and don't worry about Sheriff Collins."

"Thanks. I'll see you in a couple of hours."

Joanna spent the next two hours putting up flyers for her tai chi class. She started with the Outpouring coffee shop, the Book Nook, and the hardware store, introducing herself as she went. She put up twenty-two flyers in all. Then she was driving down Ocean Avenue and past a dozen or so small homes that had the look of something built in the 1950s.

Deputy Cowdrey's Gremlin was parked in the driveway. She parked behind it, put Rusty on a leash, and walked him down to the beach. When she returned, she saw that the deputy was sitting in the sidecar.

"Oh, hey, sorry. I just couldn't resist," he said and jumped out, looking a bit surprised when Rusty jumped in right after. She tied his leash to the grab bar and followed Chuck into his house.

"Can I get you something to drink? Coffee, or a beer?"

"No thanks," Joanna replied. "I have to confess; I'm also going to call Portland."

"No problem."

"Do you know anything about Thayer Spelling?"

"The writer who had the apartment before you, yeah. What do you want to know?"

"What can you tell me?"

"She answered an ad just like you. But she really came down to do research on the Chinese community here. She'd heard about the Chinese gold and was doing interviews when, one day, she showed up at the police station complaining about ghosts. Next thing you know, she takes off. Not a word that's she's leaving—just gone."

Joanna nodded and walked into the kitchen. The phone was on the wall next to the refrigerator. She called information to get the number for Beach Front Publishing, the company listed on the first page of the manuscript.

"Beach Front Publishing, how may I direct your call?"

"I need to speak with whoever was working with Thayer Spelling."

"One moment please."

A couple of minutes later, a different voice spoke through the line. "This is Kindle Martin. Who's this?"

Chapter Thirteen

"My name is Joanna Bright. I've come into possession of a manuscript by Thayer Spelling on the Chinese community of Dungeness Bay, and I'd like to return it to her, but I can't locate her."

"Oh really? And exactly how did you get her manuscript? I'm her editor here at Beach Front and she received a fifty-thousand-dollar advance for that story. Shortly after she deposited the advance she dropped out of sight."

"She was living above a museum in Dungeness Bay and left without notice. I was hired to take her place. I found the manuscript sitting on a desk."

"Good for you. That manuscript is the property of Beach Front Publishing. What did you say your name was?"

"Joanna Bright. But I only have half of the manuscript. I believe that the second half tells the location of hundreds of thousands of dollars worth of gold paid to the Chinese doctors by miners back then." She explained further, "That is, the doctors who owned the museum and apothecary that Thayer lived above."

There was a pause on the other end before Martin continued. "You've piqued my interest. What gold and what miners?"

"I'm sorry, my only interest is finding out what happened to Thayer Spelling and getting the partial manuscript to her. When was the last time you heard from her?"

"A few months ago. She called to acknowledge that she received the advance."

"That's about the time she disappeared from Dungeness Bay. I think something's happened to her."

"What in the world would make you say that?"

"She left without notice and took all her belongings *except* her typewriter and half the manuscript."

"Be that as it may, I hope that Thayer isn't in any kind of danger. Speaking of the manuscript, you'll need to mail that portion of the manuscript to Kindle Martin, care of Beach Front Publishing—"

"Excuse me," Joanna interrupted, "I can't do that right now. It may have clues that will lead me to Thayer's whereabouts."

"Now listen to me—"

"My attorney will be in touch, Miss Martin. Goodbye."

Joanna hung up the phone and sat down at the kitchen table, suddenly aware that Deputy Cowdrey had been standing just inside the kitchen and listening to the entire conversation.

"What makes you think that Thayer Spelling didn't just leave?"

The tone of Chuck's voice startled her.

"I don't know that for sure."

"I heard what you told Martin."

"How did you know whom I was talking to?"

Chuck held out a cordless phone.

"You have no right to listen to my calls," Joanna said indignantly.

"I have every right. You're using my phone."

Joanna turned and walked out the front door. She could hear his footfalls and knew he was following her. She marched past his Gremlin to the sidecar and unclipped Rusty from his leash. He bounded out and growled at Chuck, who drew his gun.

"Call off your dog."

Joanna clapped her hands and called his name as she climbed on the motorcycle. Rusty leaped back in the sidecar, and she started the engine, backed out of the driveway, and accelerated down the street as fast as the Ural could go. She didn't slow down until she turned onto her driveway and pulled to a stop when the graveled parking area in front of the apothecary came into sight. Two Harley motorcycles were parked behind an aging Chevy van that was backed up to the two large doors. The doors were obviously open, pulled back against the building.

She turned off the engine, leaned over, and removed her gun

from the holster under the top of the sidecar. She pulled back the slide and unclipped Rusty from his leash but told him to stay, knowing that if she called, he'd be at her side in a heartbeat.

She could hear talking in hushed voices coming from the apothecary and stepped around so the open back of the van was behind her. All she could see were two shadows moving something. She raised her gun hand, pointing it straight up, figuring she would fire a shot in the air, when someone grabbed her in a bear hug from behind. That's when her martial arts training kicked in.

She first launched a right elbow, then a left, toward her attacker's head as a distraction. Then, she bent in half, grabbed his leg, and did a somersault, rolling to the ground and taking him down with a leg lock.

"Mack, stop struggling. Joanna, let him up."

Keeping the attacker's leg locked, Joanna looked over at the smiling face of William Snow.

"Mack, this is the woman I was telling you about." Mack stopped struggling and slapped the floor several times. Joanna reluctantly released his leg.

Snow bent down and offered his hand. "That was pretty slick."

She watched as the man called Mack got up and stretched. He turned to face her and Snow and without a word, walked into the shadows.

Joanna was covered in dust and could feel a hitch where her right shoulder had hit the floor when she had somersaulted.

She walked to catch up with Snow. "All right, what's going on?"

"Mack was a field medic in our unit. The guy is fine until he sees a gun," Snow explained.

She shook her head. "So?"

"So, he's going to take care of Alex."

"What?"

"Alex is in a coma. He needs his vitals monitored and basic needs met, and Mack can see to that."

Joanna stepped past Snow into the apothecary and couldn't believe her eyes. "You brought Alex here? No, no. This place is filthy and the monitors he'll need would blow these old circuits to bits and probably burn the place down."

"We know all that. Come take a look," Snow said.

The back room was shrouded in sheets. Four monitors were plugged into a cable the size of her arm that ran out the back door.

"Where does the cable go?"

"We've set up a generator. The cot at the side is where Mack will sleep."

John walked up next to Snow.

"John, Snow, this is impossibly wrong and can't work. How did you get him out of the hospital, anyway?"

"Mack showed up and played next of kin. We loaded him into the van, and here we are."

"But the monitors, and the hospital bed," Joanna said, sweeping her hand through the air. "And all of this?"

"Mack works at the Snake Creek medical supply house in Lincoln City. It's rented. I told him you were good for it."

Joanna ran her fingers through her hair. She walked past Snow, stopped at the foot of the hospital bed. "This is crazy, just crazy."

Chapter Fourteen

Mack Masterson walked up next to Joanna at the foot of the bed and observed Alex.

"His vitals are improving. Sometimes, when the body is subject to a dramatic shock, like the fall he took, it goes into a coma—you know, like it's checking all the circuits. At this point, he's in a deep sleep and should wake up in the next twenty-four to forty-eight hours. They were going to medevac him to California tonight. We just couldn't let that happen. Snow said you felt the same way. Sorry about the bear hug. Guns just set me off."

Joanna turned and faced Mack. "How's the leg?"

"Fine. You might want to give me a minute. I've got to change his catheter bag."

Joanna nodded, hustling back out to the parking area upon hearing Rusty barking. She watched as Snow and John circled the Ural.

"Rusty, come."

John got out of the way as Rusty jumped out of the sidecar, ignored the two men, and ran to her side.

John laughed. "I'll bet this thing does sixty miles per hour wide open."

"Sixty-eight," Joanna replied. "I'll take three wheels over two any day."

Before John could react, she lurched forward and gave him a hug. "You guys aren't as tough as you look."

John broke the hug and, without a backward glance, walked away and started his classic 1948 Harley. Snow came up beside Joanna, chuckling. "I think you embarrassed him. By the way, we talked to the sheriff. He doesn't know that Alex is here."

He waved goodbye and she watched them spray gravel as they rode out of the parking lot, but didn't care. She returned to the apothecary to talk to Mack.

"Would you like to come up for dinner? I'm making chili."

"No, thank you, ma'am. If it's not too much trouble, I'd like to take my meals down here. Alex's monitors are all aligned, indicating that he's about to wake up."

Joanna threw together a batch of chili and brought down two big bowls and two beers. Mack watched her enter with the food and indicated a wheeled tray.

"He should open his eyes any time. When he does, talk about the familiar. His brain will be adjusting. If it gets overloaded, he could go back into a coma."

They ate in silence, with Mack getting up several times to adjust a monitor.

When Alex woke, Mack gave Joanna a wink.

Alex turned his head. "Mack, what are you doing here?" As if he just noticed her, Alex reached a hand out to Joanna.

....

Mack stayed through the night. The next morning, he declared Alex healed and helped Joanna walk him up the steps and into the spare bedroom. Then, he loaded the monitors and, with Joanna's help, got the hospital bed in the van.

"He's going to sleep a lot and have low energy. Feed him simple nutritious foods and take it easy on him."

Joanna balked at the last comment. "Hey, we're just friends."

Then Mack was gone.

Joanna walked into her room, picked up her journal, fluffed the pillows, and flopped onto the bed.

Dear Journal,

Less than a week in Dungeness Bay and I have a man sleeping in my spare bedroom. His name is Alex Jenner, and he drives a taxi and has been there for me on several occasions. Almost from the first day I arrived, someone has been leaving notes, telling me that I should leave. From what Alex told me, before his accident, of course, there were a lot of caretakers hired for the apothecary who reported strange sounds to the local sheriff just before they left. This does not scare me, although the brake line on my Ural motorcycle was cut. I don't believe in ghosts.

The last person to live in this apartment was a writer. She left without notice and took everything but her typewriter and a partial manuscript. I called the publisher, who said that Thayer Spelling received and deposited her advance and then dropped out of sight.

The editor at Beach Front Publishing said that because they had paid the advance, they owned the manuscript. I hung up on her because I think if I examine the portion of the manuscript I have, it may contain clues as to what happened to Thayer. I hear Alex stirring...will write later.

Joanna walked to the kitchen to make the vegetable smoothie she planned on feeding him.

When she entered his room, Alex was sitting on the side of the bed.

"Hey, you're not supposed to be getting up."

"Who says?"

"Mack said you would be low energy and sleep a lot."

"Well, my back tells me that I've been spending a lot of time in bed. I haven't tried to stand or walk, but it feels really good to be sitting up," he said, as his eyes dropped from her face to what she was holding. "I hope you don't expect me to drink that."

"I do. Mack said I should feed you nutritious food. This has got five vegetables and some protein powder in it."

She walked around the bed until she stood in front of him and held it out.

"Here. Drink up, and don't be an ingrate."

He took a drink and made a face. "Do you want to tell me how

I got here?"

Joanna remembered that Mack had said to keep the conversations simple.

Alex smiled as if he knew what Joanna was thinking. "If I get overwhelmed with your answers, I'll hold up two fingers."

"Very funny. I drove to Lincoln City to visit you and met two biker vets, William Snow and John, who were there for the same reason. Long story short, I passed out some flyers around town for the tai chi class I'm going to teach and talked Deputy Cowdrey into letting me use his phone, then I drove back here. Turns out, John, Snow, and Mack stole you out of the Lincoln City hospital and brought you here."

Alex held up two fingers. "Uh, I think I'm overwhelmed. Help me lay down."

Without waiting, he fell back.

"Are you all right?" Joanna asked in concern.

"Yeah, a little light-headed, that's all. Can you lift my legs up on the bed, and maybe pull a cover over me?"

Chapter Fifteen

Alex was asleep by the time Joanna had lifted his legs onto the bed and covered him with a light blanket. Everything was happening so fast, and now, she'd set herself up to teach a tai chi class, and the apothecary wasn't near being clean enough to take anyone on a tour through it. She was glad she had a week to tidy up.

She'd been obsessed over the partial manuscript. It was time to set it aside and focus on the apothecary. First, she needed to get rid of that hideous ottoman.

Tape measure in hand, Joanna opened the door to the lift and pulled the rope, hand over hand, bringing up the car, then locked it in place with the lever that pressed the rope against the pulley. She stepped inside and measured top to bottom front to back.

"Four feet by four feet."

Rusty crawled out from under the desk, walked over, and sniffed at the box-like car but didn't venture in.

"The ottoman is just over two feet high and three feet across. It should fit just fine," Joanna said, looking over at Rusty. "And it's not too heavy."

She slid the ottoman across the plank floor, creating some scratches, but when she got the ottoman in front of the box and pushed, the stout wooden legs hung up where the car and the floor came together.

"You're a service dog; come over here and help me," she told Rusty jokingly. Rusty just stared at her, tail wagging.

Making a face, Joanna climbed over the top of the ottoman and into the car. Scooting over on her knees, she lifted, pulled, and bounced the ottoman halfway in. All she had to do was climb over the top and out of the lift, then lift and push the ottoman the rest of the way in. But when she climbed onto the ottoman, the rope broke. The ottoman flipped up, blocking her exit, and the dumbwaiter, the ottoman, and Joanna plummeted over twenty-five feet to its landing below. When it stopped, the wood landing splintered, and the little car descended another twelve feet into the stone basement.

Rusty was frantic, running back and forth in front of the shaft, barking. After a moment, he ran into the hall and barked at the bedroom door until Alex staggered out.

"Hey, hey. Can't a guy get any sleep?" he groused, leaning against the wall. Alex watched as Rusty ran into the living room then returned and barked at him some more.

"I get it, you want me to follow."

But when Alex reached the living room, Rusty headed for the front door, barking all the way. Staggering and leaning on the wall and desk, Alex finally made his way to the front of the apartment and opened the door.

"Go do your business. Where's Joanna, anyway?"

Alex looked around the room as his vision closed in. "Guess I'm a little light-headed," he said. He leaned his back against the wall, slid to the floor, and passed out.

Rusty pounded down the steps and ran around to the front of the apothecary, but the big wooden doors were closed. He scratched at the door, alternately barking and trying to get his nose in the little space that separated the two wooden doors. Then he back-pedaled, growling and showing his teeth.

The giant door slowly swung open. Rusty poked his head in and unleashed and series of barks, like machine-gun fire, then ran across the apothecary floor to the back room where he barked down the short shaft that ended in the basement.

"Good boy."

Rusty whined and raised his head and barked at the figure that was hovering three feet above the floor.

"I'm afraid, my four-legged friend, that there is nothing I can do but show you the way," the figure said.

A small coffee table with a lamp slowly slid across the floor, revealing a steep set of stone steps. Rusty danced around, barking at the table during its unassisted movement. He ran to the edge of the steps and leaped back like he'd been faced with a snake rather than the floating image that was urging him forward.

"Come along beast, your master needs you."

With a growl and a single bark, Rusty bounded down the steps, looking back once he reached the bottom. The figure was gone.

Joanna blinked awake at the sound of the voice urging Rusty on. "Here boy," she said, trying to move.

The weight of the lift and the ottoman, which lay across a long plank, pinned Joanna's legs to the stone floor. She reached around the back of her head, which had struck on the floor when she had crashed, but her hand came away dry and all she felt was a very sensitive goose egg.

Light streamed in from the shaft and down the narrow steps. Joanna craned her neck to look around at the steps. For a moment, she thought she saw a figure standing there but couldn't hold her head up any longer and rested it on the floor.

Rusty had stopped barking and waited for a command, looking from Joanna to the figure, which had reappeared on the steps.

"I am afraid that your four-legged mongrel will have to free you. There is nothing I can do."

Startled, Joanna called out, "Hello? Please come around where I can see you."

"As you wish."

The figure floated around to the opposite side of the shaft and above the dumbwaiter car and the ottoman. He wore a long happi coat that would have hung down to his ankles if he had any. His left arm was in the right sleeve and his right arm was in the left sleeve. A long queue of braided hair was hanging down the middle of his back.

Joanna peered into the gloom. "Who are you, and why are you dressed that way?"

"I am Doc Hay," the figure responded.

Rusty ran back and forth as if sizing up the situation, then jumped up on the plank that supported the ottoman. His 100 pounds flipped it off to one side, allowing Joanna to wiggle out from under the boards.

"Good boy Rusty; good boy."

He came over by her side and she pulled him into a hug.

"Judging from his lack of aggression, I believe your dog Rusty has adjusted to my appearance."

Joanna stood up on wobbly legs to let in more light and get a better look at the shimmering image.

Chapter Sixteen

"Doc Hay. That's what you called yourself, and that's what the miners called you. My god, you're dead."

"I have left this mortal coil, but not terra firma."

"You're a ghost?"

"In China, the term 'ghost' has so many negative mind traps. I prefer spirit."

Joanna looked around at the odd platforms that lined the walls and the long table in the middle of the room.

"What is this place?"

"At first, this was an opium den. When Long On joined me in medicine, this became a clinic for the very sick," Doc Hay said, waving an arm to indicate one wall. "These platforms were covered with cotton batting and hay and were the beds."

Still confounded, Joanna asked, "If you're a ghost—ah, spirit—why are you here? How can I see you?"

"I am not certain. I know that you are the first person to come down here in over seventy-five years. When you broke through, it allowed me to move around my herb shop, but I don't believe that I can travel outside this structure. Why you can see me may have something to do with hitting your head."

Joanna looked around. "What did you use for light down here?"

"Lanterns."

"You said you couldn't help me. Does that mean you can't interact with people?"

"I have limitations. When I saw that you were trapped and possibly injured, I was able to push the front door open and then again move the low table and lantern, revealing the stairs. I believe that my emotional state and concern over your situation allowed me to affect those solid objects," he explained before disappearing.

Joanna reached around and touched the goose-egg-sized bump

on the back of her head and wondered if she'd been hallucinating.

"Rusty, just tell me that you saw Doc Hay too."

She was startled when Doc Hay's apparition reappeared just inches in front of her.

"There is a person in the apartment who could use your assistance."

"Come on, Rusty. Upstairs, back to the apartment."

When Joanna reached the landing at the top of the steps, she noticed that the door was open. She slowed her pace, and cautiously alert, stepped into the living room.

Doc Hay appeared and pointed. "He is in the kitchen."

She moved to the kitchen door and could hear running water. She entered to see Alex leaning over the sink.

She came up next to him, placing an arm on his back.

"Alex, are you all right?"

"Yeah, just splashing water on my face. Where did you go? Rusty needed to get out and do his business. I opened the door for him, then blacked out."

Joanna helped him into a kitchen chair, then pulled one around to face him and sat.

Alex rubbed his temples. "I feel kind of foggy and light-headed, but you look like you've seen a ghost."

"I was in the lift when the rope broke. I crashed and was trapped in the old basement. I hit my head pretty hard, and think I've been hallucinating," she said. She took Alex's hand and guided it around to the bump on the back of her head.

"Lean down and let me take a look."

Joanna leaned forward and rested her forehead on Alex's knees. He parted her hair, exposing a raised purple bump, and gingerly touched it with one finger.

"Sit up and look me in the eye."

She pushed against his legs to sit up straight, and locked eyes with him.

"Are you seeing double?"

"No."

"What's the name of your service dog, and what's my name?"

"Your name is Rusty, and the dog's name is Alex," she said, laughing. When she stopped laughing she started crying.

He held one of her hands, saying, "Hey. You're okay, and I'm feeling a lot better."

Joanna sniffed once, then wiped her eyes. "Sorry. It's just that I don't think I'm okay."

He tilted his head. "You seem fine."

"I think it's just that so much has happened since I arrived in Dungeness Bay," she said, looked away, then back at Alex. "When I was down in the basement, my legs were pinned by the weight of the ottoman I was trying to move into the dumbwaiter car. I don't know how, but Rusty found me and so did Doc Hay."

"Who?"

"The ghost of Ing Hay—the guy who owned this place. Doc Hay was his nickname."

Alex smiled and slowly nodded his head. "Okay, what did this Doc Hay have to say?"

Joanna's eyes flooded with tears that threatened to run over her cheeks.

"He told me that someone in the apartment needed my help, and when I got here, he pointed and said you were in the kitchen."

"How did you get out from under the weight of the dumbwaiter car?"

"Rusty jumped on a plank and the ottoman slid to one side, taking the weight off so I could free my legs."

"No ghost there, just one smart dog."

"But how did he get the big wooden door open?"

"Come on," Alex said reassuringly, "you know how dogs are. If we go down there, we'd see a lot of scratches on the bottom of the door. It probably opened just far enough for him to get in."

Joanna made a face. The steps that led down to the basement were concealed by a low table with a lantern and attached to a board. There was no way Rusty could have known to move the table.

Alex got up and shuffled to the kitchen door. "Is your ghost here now?"

Joanna looked around. "I don't think so."

"Do you think Rusty saw your ghost?"

"Yes, and stop calling him my ghost."

"Maybe you *have* been hallucinating. I understand that you found Gus's body and were pretty battered by the storm that first day, not to mention that your truck was crushed by a tree."

"Yeah, and how about all those notes telling me to leave this place?"

Alex walked back to the kitchen table and sat down hard. "I know I'm adding to the burden you were under before you got to know me. I'm past needing a nurse now, and it's just a matter of getting my strength and energy back. If you help me out to my car, I'm sure I can manage to get home."

Joanna snorted. "Right, if you don't pass out during the drive. No. Until you can navigate the stairs and race Rusty down to the beach, it's here you'll stay.

Chapter Seventeen

"I want you to think about that offer. You're a single woman with a man under the same roof. Joanna, this is a small town. People will talk."

Joanna stared at Alex, pursing her lips. "Fine," she finally agreed. "As you probably already know, the stipend the city is paying me doesn't amount to a row of beans. If it'll make you and the rest of the town feel better, you can rent the room."

"Fair enough, and you can also consider me security, keeping you safe from your ghost and whoever is sending you those nasty notes. Hmm, we share the kitchen and the bathroom. What do you want for rent?"

"No charge until your energy returns, and that will take care of my guilt. If you hadn't been helping me clean, you never would have taken that fall. Once you're up to it, you can rewire the apothecary. What do you say?"

"Deal."

They locked eyes at the sound of a car coming up the drive. Joanna helped Alex up, and together they walked to the kitchen window that overlooked the parking area.

"It's the sheriff. I guess he didn't believe John and Snow," Alex said, and moved around the kitchen wall for support, making his way out to the landing.

"Hello Alex. I trust you're recovering from your fall?"

"I am. You'll have to help me down the stairs."

"I'm not here for you. I need to speak with Joanna. Can you send her down? There's something in the apothecary I want to show her."

Joanna had been listening and stepped past Alex. She descended the steps, followed by Rusty.

Sheriff Collins eyed Rusty. "Can you tie up your dog? My deputy said he attacked him."

She walked around to the side of the building where she had parked the sidecar and tied Rusty to the rear tire. She came back around, her ears burning, to face the sheriff.

"Just so you know, your deputy eavesdropped on a private phone conversation I was having and pulled his gun on me."

"Well, Chuck is a pretty simple guy," the sheriff said, looking directly at Joanna. "You must have done something to provoke him."

"I can see where this is going. Why are you here?" Joanna demanded.

"No, I don't think you see at all, but I'll try and put things in order for you," he said, and pulled open the big wooden door to the apothecary. "I want to show you something."

Joanna followed him into the apothecary. The sheriff stopped and looked up at the loft.

"What?"

"That was quite a fall Alex took. It could have killed him," he said. He bent down and picked up a portion of the rail that had broken away, and held it out for Joanna to see. "Now does that look broken to you?"

She turned it over and examined each end. "No."

"Exactly, it's been cut partway through. I was here—"

She cut him off. "Snooping around."

"Well, that, and I was curious. I've never been to this old apothecary. You know what else I found?"

She followed the sheriff into a small side room where the books of herbal remedies were kept and pulled out half a ream of unbound paper.

"Please notice that this is in English and starts on page one-hundred and thirty-one. I believe this is half of the manuscript written by Thayer Spelling. Speaking of Mrs. Spelling, I got a call from her publisher explaining that you called inquiring about her whereabouts, stating that you had a portion of her manuscript. I believe you spoke to Kindle Martin. She was quite upset. Apparently, when she explained that she had advanced fifty thousand dollars to Mrs. Spelling for a story and, therefore, that the manuscript belonged to Beach Front Publishing, you hung up on her."

Joanna reached for the manuscript, but the sheriff pulled it just out of reach.

"I think you had the entire manuscript. That's why you didn't want to return it, and the reason this half is down here is that you were using it to guide you to what the locals call miners' gold."

"I had no idea that half of the manuscript was down here, or anywhere, for that matter," Joanna argued. "I'll get you the first half. Go ahead and mail it back."

The sheriff shook his head. "I don't think so; it's evidence."

"Of what?"

"I said I'd put things in order."

"Get to the point," Joanna said impatiently.

"Perhaps we should go upstairs so Alex can hear what I have to say."

"I'm right here, Sheriff."

The two of them turned to face Alex, who was leaning heavily on the big wooden door.

"Here's what I think. Gus Hasselbacker was working closely with Thayer Spelling in her history of Dungeness Bay. When you answered the ad, applying for the position as caretaker of the apothecary, you did a little research on the area and were intrigued by the story about miners' gold. You discovered in your research that a woman had been sent down by a Portland publisher to write a story that would be the basis for a documentary.

"You first made contact with Gus over the phone. He told you he'd been working closely with the writer, Thayer Spelling. At some point, after you'd been hired, you planned on contacting Gus again, asking him to meet you at the apothecary museum and if he could possibly bring the manuscript because you'd love to know the history of Dungeness Bay and the apothecary. You met poor Gus, and under the cover of the storm, something happened. Perhaps he decided he shouldn't be giving you the manuscript, that he hadn't made a copy and didn't want to give you the original. You took it, and when he demanded it back, you took his cane away and struck him with a killing blow to the head."

Alex laughed. "You've been reading too many mysteries, Sheriff."

"Just hear me out, Alex. From the moment Ms. Bright arrived, you've been helping her get settled. You went out and got her suitcases, you provided her with transportation, and then you brought over your vacuum cleaner for her. And when you volunteered to help her clean up down here, she became afraid that you might stumble on the hiding place for the gold, so she cut partway through the rail of the loft, knowing that, at some point, you'd lean on it. It would break away, and you, Alex, would fall to your death."

With that, the sheriff pulled handcuffs out from the back of his belt. "Joanna Bright, you had both means and motive, and the storm served as an opportunity for you to kill Gus. I'm arresting you for the murder of Gus Hasselbacker and the attempted murder of Alex Jenner."

Sheriff Collins grabbed Joanna's right arm, twisting it behind her back, and clicked a handcuff around her wrist, then did the same to her left arm. He turned her around and walked her to his cruiser, reading her Miranda rights.

"Joanna Bright, you have the right to remain silent and refuse to answer questions. Anything you say may be used against you in a court of law. You have the right to consult an attorney before speaking to the police and to have an attorney present during questioning now or in the future."

Joanna looked back and yelled out, "Alex, call Ned Branch, my attorney. He's in Pacific Grove, California. Tell him everything."

Alex sagged against the door, refusing to believe the sheriff's story. When he heard a whine, he pulled himself up straight. Using the side of the old building, he walked around, following the whine.

"Rusty."

He stumbled to the Ural, coaxed the service dog into the sidecar, and felt around the base of the gas tank for the spare key.

"Hang on buddy. We're going to my bachelor pad to make a phone call."

Fueled by an adrenaline rush, Alex made it up his driveway but collapsed as his vision began to close in, just making it through the front door. He was brought around by something cold and wet on his cheek.

"Okay boy. Good boy, Rusty."

Leaning on the wall, he made it to his computer room, slumped into the captain's chair, and pounded on the space bar until the screen came up. He Googled Ned Branch of Pacific Grove, California, and then grabbed his landline and made the call. He'd need some support if he was going to make it through this. Alex made a second call, then toppled off the chair, unconscious.

....

After their conversation, Ned immediately called the Dungeness Bay Police Department, talked to the sheriff, and wired bail. After he hung up, he canceled his appointments for the next three days and set off for Dungeness Bay.

Chapter Eighteen

Sheriff Collins walked up to the door where female prisoners were kept and knocked twice.

"Are you on the pot or anything?" he called out.

"No, Sheriff."

He opened the door and stepped to one side. "It seems your attorney has paid your bail. Would you like a ride back to your apartment? I could give Chuck a call."

"No thanks," Joanna muttered.

"You're still a person of interest, so don't leave town."

Without a word, she walked out of the little brick police department.

Ears burning, she headed down the sidewalk, looking at all the businesses that had closed for the night and realizing how alone she was.

The light in the Chocolate Factory was on. Ms. Posey was probably creating another vat of chocolate. Joanna paused to take in the display at the Book Nook and was shocked by her reflection in the window. Her hair was a mess. She straightened her blouse, took a deep calming breath, and moved on down the sidewalk, where the light streamed out into the street from the Outpouring Coffee House and Café, open until nine. Thanks to the sheriff, she'd missed dinner and had a gnawing hunger. She'd been in the Outpouring once before when she handed out flyers for her tai chi class to the owner, Cheryl.

The coffee shop looked more like an old-fashioned soda fountain parlor. Twelve stools lined a long Formica countertop. Orders for coffee, soup, and sandwiches were made at the bar, and the remainder of the roughly five-hundred-square-foot room was filled with tables—no booths. The place was empty. Cheryl, the owner, was behind the bar, and she was happy to have the coffee shop to herself after a busy day of serving tourists.

Joanna walked to a corner of the dining area. She turned her back to the big-picture window and bar, reached into her bra, and removed the twenty-dollar bill she kept there. She flashed back on how her mother had always told her that no matter where she went, or whom she went with, she should always have some money on hand. It was one of those funny habits that had paid off more than once.

"Hi Cheryl, how's business?"

Cheryl Chin stood just over five feet. She sported a bright smile and jet-black hair that framed her heart-shaped face. She was always dressed to the nines and bubbled with energy.

"Really good! I had to call in an extra worker to help handle all the tourists. If I'm not mistaken, Lisa Posey over at the Chocolate Factory had the same problem." Just then, the little bell over the door came to life, and the two looked over. "Speak of the devil."

Lisa Posey walked in, grinning. "I heard that."

"Have you two met?" Cheryl asked.

"Joanna, right?" Lisa said. "Your flyer said you are starting the tai chi class. Are you going to hold the classes up at the old herb shop?"

Before Joanna could respond, Cheryl reached out and put a hand on Joanna's arm. "We saw you riding in the back seat of the sheriff's cruiser. Is everything all right?"

Joanna looked from one woman to the other. "Truth: Since the day I arrived, I've been caught up in a whirlwind of the unexpected."

Lisa sat on a stool next to Joanna. "The night of the storm, Deputy Chuckles came into the shop, dripping from all points. He bought a pound of the dark chocolate bridge mix and said the new caretaker of the museum found the body of Gus Hasselbacker."

Joanna moaned. "That's when it all started. Now the sheriff thinks I killed him."

"You're kidding," Cheryl said, her mouth agape.

"No joke. That's why you saw me in his cruiser."

"Sheriff Collins is a sad and angry man," Cheryl said. She walked to the front of the shop and flipped the sign on the door so it read "Closed." "What say I put on a fresh pot of coffee?"

"I haven't eaten since lunch, and I'm starved. Is there anything you could just pull out of the freezer?"

"How about tomato and roasted red pepper soup?"

"Is there enough for two?" Lisa piped in.

"Oh yeah, just give me a minute to warm it up," Cheryl said and bustled into the kitchen.

Joanna made a face. "Why did Cheryl say that the sheriff's angry?"

"He's got an older brother in Portland with Lou Gehrig's disease—you know, ALS. He took early retirement so he could take care of him, and keep him out of a care center. He was still on contract with the city when the budget cuts hit, and the entire police force was cut loose. They brought him back, from what I hear, at half pay, and now his brother is in a special nursing home and it's costing him a fortune."

Cheryl pushed through the kitchen's swinging doors with three bowls of steaming soup on a tray.

"Belly up, ladies."

Joanna felt her eyes burn with unshed tears. "You know, this is the nicest thing that's happened to me since I arrived in Dungeness Bay."

For a moment all was silent, then Cheryl pulled out a spoon, napkin, and crackers from under the counter. "Come on, my soup isn't that good."

All three laughed, and Joanna smiled into her soup, thinking that it really was that good.

Lisa finished her soup and pushed her bowl to one side. "Joanna, it sounds like a lot has happened to you since arriving in Dungeness Bay. Most all of us were glad to hear that the city had hired a caretaker slash tour guide for the old herb shop—"

"What do you mean, most?" Joanna interrupted.

"It was the mayor's idea to give the apothecary one more chance as a tourist attraction."

Chapter Nineteen

Lisa looked over at Cheryl, who gave her a nod. "The property on the bluff where the apothecary sits was going to be turned into a park, but Mayor Ritter brought the businesses together and convinced them it would help bring money into the town."

"I had no idea," Joanna said.

"I hate to break up a good thing, but I'm opening tomorrow, so I've gotta get going," Lisa said.

"I'm marooned in town," Joanna said.

"Say no more," Lisa said. "I'd be happy to take you back to your apartment."

When they rolled onto the gravel drive, Joanna asked her to wait while she went up to her apartment. Moments later, she came down the stairs, climbed back in Lisa's SUV, and took a calming breath.

"Do you know Alex Jenner?"

"The taxi guy? Sure, everyone knows Alex. What's up?"

"He was helping me clean the apothecary and took a fall from the loft. He was in the hospital for a while but he's been recovering in my guest room. Well, he's gone now. When the sheriff arrested me, I asked Alex to call my attorney, and I think he may have gone home to make the call."

"Got it. I think I know where he lives," Lisa said as she accelerated back into town. "Alex is a really nice guy. Are the two of you a thing?"

Joanna blushed. "No. At least, I don't think so. I can't speak for Alex, though he's been hanging around a lot. Right now, I'm just concerned, that's all."

Lisa stopped in front of a small house. "I could stick around if you'd like?"

"Thank you, but I'll be okay. It looks like he took the Ural for some reason."

The two women paused their conversation at the sound of a dog barking.

"He must have brought Rusty with him," Joanna said, and gave Lisa a hug. "I'll be fine, really."

Joanna walked up the two steps to the door and found it unlocked. When she opened it, Rusty ran to her side and licked her hand.

"Good boy, Rusty. Where's Alex?" Joanna spun a slow circle." This place is tiny. You inherited money, why would you live here?"

She walked down a short hall and entered the only bedroom.

When she first entered the room, she didn't see Alex, but when she walked over to the computer, she gasped. "Oh my gosh." She bent down and straightened out Alex's legs as she rolled him on his back, freeing up both his arms, then took his pulse.

There was no way to get his limp form on the bed, so she pulled off the bedspread, covered him up, then decided to pull off his shoes and socks. She'd noticed he wore a belt and decided that it might be restrictive or binding. She unbuckled it, accidentally unsnapping the top button of his pants.

"Oops," Joanna said sheepishly. With Alex fully covered, Joanna reached under the bedspread and grabbed the cuff of each pant leg, gently tugging until she was able to pull his pants free. She threw them under the computer desk, then blushed and laughed when she noticed that his boxers had come off with his pants.

Joanna stood with her hands on her hips and stared at the bed. "No sheets or pillows." She walked to the tiny closet, opening it and peering inside. "No clothes on hangers and no linens. All right Alex, you've got some explaining to do."

Rusty followed her to the kitchen, where she found the cupboards bare, then went down the rather short hall to the bathroom, where she discovered a sheet rolled up alongside a couple of towels, which she carried back to the bedroom.

"What do you think, Rusty?" she said, walking over to give Alex's foot a nudge with her shoe. With a sigh, she stripped down to her underwear and climbed on the bed, using the towels for a pillow, and pulled the sheet up to her chin. She stared at the ceiling, wondering what could possibly top this, then drifted off to sleep.

Joanna hadn't noticed that none of the windows had curtains, including the bedroom. When the sun broke through the morning fog, it streaked across the little bedroom, waking her from a sound sleep. She slipped out of bed, wrapping the sheet around her like a toga, but Alex was gone.

"Now what?" She kept one eye on the door while she dressed. When she stepped out of the room, the aroma of coffee wafted down the hall. She walked to the kitchen barefoot. Alex met her at the kitchen door with a sixteen-ounce cup of coffee bearing the Outpouring logo.

"Coffee?" Alex offered. "I hope you take it black?"

"Thanks, have a seat. I've got a few questions," Joanna said.

"Yeah, me too."

She took a sip. "You go first."

"I've got a vague memory of talking to an attorney named Branch. You're here, so I assume that he paid your bail. I called the doctor who oversaw my treatment when I was in a coma. He said I'm passing out because I'm thinking too much. He said my brain is still trying to work things out, and when it's overloaded, it shuts down the body."

Alex looked away, then took a long drink of coffee. He locked eyes with Joanna. "When I woke up, I couldn't find my pants."

She blushed, then smiled and took a couple of sips of the hot coffee while she decided what to say. "I got it in my head that your belt and pants might be binding. Your boxers came off with the pants, but you were covered the entire time."

He gave a short, sharp laugh. "That's a relief. Now, you had some questions for me?"

"There are no sheets or bedding of any kind. There are no dishes. Tell me you don't live here."

Chapter Twenty

Alex nodded. "Okay, I don't live here. I own three rentals, and this was the closest and unoccupied. The renter had just moved out so there was still a phone and electricity." Alex stood and stretched. "I took Rusty for a walk this morning. How did you find the house?"

"After the sheriff turned me loose, I met Lisa Posey and she gave me a ride. She said she thought she knew where you lived."

"Lisa owns the chocolate factory and does real estate on the side. She sold me this house and two others."

Joanna stood. "I should get back to my apartment. I want to clean the apothecary before my first tai chi class. But if I take the Ural, you'd be stranded. Even so, I don't know that I want to leave you here alone. Why don't you and Rusty hop in the sidecar and I'll drive us back to my apartment? You can just hang out—no pressure, just let your brain recuperate."

Alex sat back down. "The only way I'm going to let that happen is if you let me pay you."

"Alex, I appreciate what you're saying, but I don't need the money. I inherited a large sum when my husband passed away and sold a physical therapy business when I left the Monterey Peninsula. Look, I'm in need of a shower and a change of clothes. Come along and I'll fix breakfast, and we can continue this conversation on a full stomach."

After Alex agreed, the two of them exited the house. When Joanna climbed on the motorcycle, Rusty hopped in the sidecar, next to Alex, and looked up with his excited face.

It was early, and Joanna felt a sense of relief that she wouldn't be dealing with tourist traffic. Twenty minutes later, she pulled onto the gravel parking area in front of the apothecary next to the sheriff's cruiser, less the sheriff. She walked over and pulled a note from under the windshield wiper. Her name was in bold letters at the top.

Alex slowly climbed out of the sidecar and walked over. "What does it say?"

"On the beach. We need to talk, please come alone. JC."

"More problems?"

"I don't think so. Can you make the stairs alone?"

"No problem. Rusty, come on boy."

"Rusty stays with me," Joanna interjected.

"All right. Don't be long. I'll get breakfast started."

With Rusty at her side, Joanna walked to the edge of the bluff and scanned the beach until she spotted a lone figure sitting on a log just out of the tide's reach.

The two made their way down the switchback trail that led to the beach. She was surprised that, when Rusty ran ahead, the figure didn't move.

"Sheriff Collins?"

"You alone?" the sheriff asked.

"Yeah, what do you want?" Joanna walked around to face the sheriff. She was surprised to see that his face was drawn and his mouth was turned down; his eyes looked sad.

"Are you okay?"

"No. I resigned my position as sheriff and the city council has accepted my resignation."

She relaxed and glanced over at Rusty, who was playing tag with the tide.

"You probably know about my brother. The whole town knows."

"ALS. Lisa Posey told me."

"I'm moving back to Portland to pull him out of that damned care facility and take him home to die."

"Sheriff—Jesse—I'm so sorry."

"Thank you, but I didn't ask you to meet me so I could tell you my problems," the sheriff said. "First, I owe you an apology. I know that I've jumped to conclusions on several occasions, but I just can't let this business with Gus disappear with my absence, and that's what will happen." He looked up at Joanna. "I've submitted a report about my assumptions concerning you and the death of Gus Hasselbacker to the state district attorney. I've received notification that they've placed it on a docket and will be sending down a prosecutorial investigator in ten days."

Joanna was stunned and stepped back, letting the tide roll across her feet up to her ankles.

"How could you? How could the district attorney even consider a report that's filled with innuendo, guesses, and assumptions?"

"Gus was a friend. I'm hoping that the cause of his untimely death will be exposed, and the guilty party brought to justice. I could not in good conscious let the cause of his death go unsolved. The clock's ticking, Joanna. I suggest that you find out who killed Gus and produce enough evidence to convince the district attorney of your innocence."

"That's it, then. Who will take your place as sheriff?"

"I'm leaving tomorrow. Chuck Cowdrey will be interim sheriff until someone else can be brought in."

She slapped her side as she turned to leave. "Rusty."

Rusty danced around the incoming tide, then ran to her side when she walked up the beach.

The sheriff turned. "Joanna, greed is the mastermind. Suspect everyone, trust no one."

She kept walking, raising a hand in the air as an acknowledgment of his comment.

When she reached the top of the bluff, she could smell coffee. Rusty broke away, and when she reached the front of the apothecary, his nose was already buried in a bowl of kibble. She followed the aroma of freshly perked coffee and a slight scent of something else. Alex was leaning on the rail with a cup of coffee. She couldn't restrain a smile and scratched Rusty between the ears as he ate before she finally climbed the stairs.

"I hope you don't mind. I thought we could eat on the landing," Alex said, gesturing. A small coffee table was set, the plates covered.

"What's on the menu?"

"Lots of carbs and fat. Bacon, eggs, and hash browns."

They sat on the platform, facing each other, separated by the food-laden coffee table.

"Alex, I have a question. Your answer has to be absolutely honest because however you reply, it will change everything."

"This has something to do with your meeting the sheriff, doesn't it?"

"Everything. Please, promise me that you won't take this the wrong way."

Alex set down the mug of coffee he'd been holding with both hands and stood. "Maybe I should just leave."

"Please, no. Stay with me on this."

He sat down, folding his legs and picking up his coffee. "Ask your damn question."

"Collins is no longer sheriff. Before resigning, he filed a report with the state district attorney naming me as the possible murderer of Gus Hasselbacker. The state's sending down an investigator in ten days.

"Alex, as I walked away, Collins said to trust no one. I need you with me on this and I need to know that I can trust you. Tell me that you've had nothing to do with the notes telling me to leave, that you had nothing to do with Gus's murder."

Chapter Twenty-one

Rusty came bounding up the stairs and lay next to Joanna, just as Alex got up without a word and walked into the apartment.

She wrapped an arm around Rusty's neck and pulled him in tight. "I guess we're on our own."

No sooner had she finished verbalizing her worst fear than Alex emerged with a steaming pot of coffee. "Refill?"

Joanna looked up, smiling to hide her teary eyes and burning ears. "Please."

Alex refilled her mug and put the pot down, then took a deep breath before speaking. "I have every reason to be resentful, insulted, and angry. But I'm not really into riding an emotional roller coaster of game playing."

Filled with relief, Joanna stood and lunged forward, wrapping Alex in a hug. "Thank you."

After a moment, he stepped back and held her at arm's length. "What can I do?"

"I won't ask you to make decisions or take control in any way. Just be my sounding board."

He laughed. "After everything you've been through since arriving at Dungeness Bay, I'd say you're the most grounded, self-sufficient woman I've ever met."

Joanna gave a short bow and sat back down, smiling.

Alex removed the covers from the various plates. "Let's dig in before everything gets cold."

After the two had their fill, Joanna watched Alex carry the plates into the apartment, feeling lighthearted. Picking up the mugs and coffee pot, she followed him into the kitchen.

"Wash or dry?"

In answer, Alex turned on the water and picked up the sponge.

"I passed out twenty-two flyers for my tai chi class, so I can expect two or three people to show up," Joanna said conversationally.

"I don't think so. The town's bound to be abuzz with curiosity about the new caretaker of the old apothecary."

"We'll see," Joanna said. "Right now, I have to clean and get ready for whoever responds. I need a table. You know, one of those six-foot folding tables."

"I can get one from the hardware store," Alex said. "Are you going to need one of those commercial coffee urns, and maybe some Styrofoam cups?"

"Paper cups, not Styrofoam, and something to heat water for tea. You feel all right to drive into town?"

"Honestly, I feel like I'm closing in on normal—like the fog is finally lifting. I'll go now."

Joanna watched Alex descend the steps and climb into his taxi, then, with Rusty at her side, walked into the apartment, down the hall to her room, and picked up her journal. She returned to the living room and slumped into the club chair, opening the journal to the next empty page.

Dear Journal,

So much has happened in the past two days. I've been arrested on a murder charge, but the most exciting event has been with Alex Jenner. When I lost K. C., I thought I would never have another man in my life. I thought that at fifty-two, I was finished with relationships. I have to be strong and not pull Alex close to make him stay. My yesterdays are all wrapped up and put away. Is this the way it's going to be, keeping this man at arm's length, guided by my head while ignoring my heart? Perhaps time and events will position Alex closer in my life.

I can't believe that I'm accused of murder. What did Sheriff Collins say—the clock is ticking? So, it's up to me to find out who killed Gus Hasselbacker. Collins's parting words were that greed is the mastermind. Early on, Collins said I had means, motive, and opportunity. So, it's a puzzle then. I need to create a list of people I know who seem driven by greed.

Joanna paused from her writing and looked at Rusty, who was curled up in his usual spot under the desk, then began to write on a clean page, all the time wondering who could possibly be so driven by greed that they would kill.

She headed the page *Suspects* and started with the mayor:

Mayor Calvin Ritter gathered signatures, enough to save the apothecary from being torn down. Why?

Sheriff Collins is leaving the area, so he's off the list.

Alex has pledged his loyalty, not in so many words, but I trust him.

Deputy Chuck Cowdrey, now sheriff—seemed angry, lives in a rundown bungalow.

John, William Snow. Did they really come all the way from California to check up on Alex? Snow said that Alex was helping Gus financially. Was greed their true motivation for the visit?

Joanna set down her pen, reread her list of suspects, and shook her head. "Kind of a short list with so many unknowns."

She thought about Alex and began to write again.

> *God knows that Alex has had plenty of opportunities to come on to me. He seems caring but perhaps a bit restrained. Is he repulsed by all the problems I've encountered since arriving at Dungeness Bay? He's commented on my, how did he put it, grounded and self-sufficient nature. Should I open up and be more vulnerable? I promised that I wouldn't ask him to step in and take control of my situation, that I only needed a sounding board.*

He was in the first Gulf War and said he was twenty-two then. That would put his birthday in 1968, making him my senior by one year, unlike K. C., who was thirteen years older. And what about his PTSD? Is he afraid to approach me in a romantic way? Should I make the first move?

The sound of a car driving across the gravel and Rusty climbing out from under the desk brought Joanna out of her musings.

She rushed into the bedroom and stashed the journal under her mattress before walking out to the landing at the top of the stairs, where Rusty was waiting.

"Hello, can I help you?" she asked the man standing outside.

"Alex sent me with the table and paper cups you wanted."

Joanna hurried down the steps, surprised when a woman got out of the passenger side of the pickup.

"I'm Joanna Bright."

The man stepped forward, hand extended. "I'm Eric Ward. I own the hardware store, and this is my wife, Helen."

Joanna shook his hand. "Pleased to meet you."

Eric and Helen looked to be in their late sixties, maybe seventies. Both were lean and sported gray hair.

"Let me give you a hand with the table," Joanna said, following him around to the back of the truck.

Helen walked over and patted Rusty on the head. "I saw your flyers for the tai chi class. Do you need any help cleaning?"

"I'm afraid the place is covered with a layer of dust," Joanna admitted.

Chapter Twenty-two

"This place has been shut up for a long time," Helen said. "That writer woman was the last person to live in the upstairs apartment. I don't think she touched the herb shop at all. Anyway, I brought several hand vacuums, good for getting into small places."

Erick came over. "I brought some butcher paper to cover the table. What are you going to use the table for? It won't take much weight."

"I have a line of herbal teas, and thought I'd put them out for anyone who shows up to try."

"I'll set the table up on the other side of the doors. You can move it any place you want, but you'll have to weigh down the paper to keep it from blowing away," Eric said.

Helen helped Joanna open the doors and fold them back.

"Is there a back door?" she asked.

Joanna pointed to a short hall with shelves on both sides. "Right through there."

"If you don't mind, I'll open the door and see if we can get rid of decades of stale and musty air."

Eric followed his wife partway into the herb shop, stopped, and looked around, seeming to think out loud. "I'd say about two thousand square feet and maybe a couple hundred upstairs."

"I guess. I don't really know," Joanna said.

"Do you mind if I wander around a bit?"

"Not at all," she said. She watched as he walked away. Eric pulled a screwdriver from a back pocket and stabbed at some of the supporting beams and planks.

Helen walked up with a hand vac.

Joanna motioned to Eric. "What's he doing?"

Helen laughed. "Eric used to be a home inspector. He's checking for dry rot."

Both women turned at the sound of a car on the gravel drive.

"That must be Alex," Joanna said, but stopped when she walked out of the herb shop. The BMW that had driven up didn't belong to Alex.

Ned rushed out of his car. "Joanna!" he said. "I hadn't heard from you since I wired your bail. I was concerned. I didn't know where to start looking and stopped for coffee. When I mentioned your name to the manager, she drew me a map on a napkin."

"I'm sorry I haven't gotten back to you, Ned. Things have been kind of hectic."

He looked past her. "Is this where you're living?"

"Upstairs."

Ned flinched when Rusty licked his hand. "We need to talk."

"Honestly, this isn't the best time," Joanna said, looking apologetic. "I've got until next week to get this place ship-shape for my tai chi class."

"Joanna, for crying out loud. Sheriff Collins called me last night. He said he submitted a report to the state district attorney indicating you as a person of interest in the murder of Gus Hasselbacker." Ned shook his head. "You've got until next week to put together enough evidence to convince the state that you're not the killer."

"Ned, calm down. I've already journaled four suspects."

"The state isn't going to want to read your journal. Come back to California with me. I'll claim protective custody based on the threatening notes Alex said you've been receiving, and we'll put together a defense and meet the state head-on."

"I can't do that Ned."

"Look Joanna, the Oregon DA is sending down an investigator who will probably be equipped with an arrest warrant in his back pocket. Unless you can point out the killer based on solid evidence, he'll swear out the warrant and take you back to Salem in handcuffs, and I'll be digging you out of a hole—if that's even possible at that point."

"Most of the sheriff's assertions are unsubstantiated—pure speculation. A judge would never sign an arrest warrant based on insufficient evidence," Joanna argued.

"Maybe not, but something in the sheriff's report triggered a response from the DA's office, so you had better believe they're going to be taking this seriously."

"Then get a copy of that report and let me know what the trigger was."

Ned rubbed his temple. "There's nothing here for you, Joanna. Come back with me to Monterey."

"I can't go back. Dungeness Bay is my new start."

"What kind of a start? The day you arrived; you found a body. You've been accused of murder, arrested, made friends with a Gulf War veteran suffering from PTSD, and it looks like you've taken in a stray dog. And, for God's sake, look where you're living."

"That's enough Ned. I know you have my best interests at heart, but I want you to leave."

Eric stepped up, next to Joanna. "I believe the lady asked you to go."

Ned threw his hands up and walked back to his car. "K. C. always said you were hardheaded, and once you made up your mind, there was no changing it. He was right. Good luck, Joanna."

She stood like a statue and watched Ned's BMW accelerate up the driveway. When it was out of sight, she took a long, slow breath, then turned to face Eric. "I'm so sorry that you had to hear all that."

"Don't give it a second thought."

Helen came up beside her and nodded for Eric to leave. "How about you show me your apartment? I'm really curious."

As she walked up the stairs, Joanna wondered if she should have taken Ned's advice. Was this just a rough start or a mistake that she would regret for the rest of her life?

Chapter Twenty-three

The morning fog burned off at 10:30, leaving only a slight breeze. Alex had been the perfect helpmate, setting up the table, the hot water urn, and the cups. He even helped her lay out her teas, then claimed he was tired and went up to his room to take a nap.

The flyer had said the introduction to tai chi class would begin at 11:00. Joanna was wishing someone would show up early, and her wish came true when Lisa Posey pulled into the parking area.

Joanna walked up and greeted her as she climbed out of her SUV.

"Thank you for coming," she said, giving her a quick hug. "I just hope you aren't the only one."

"Helen said you had a line of teas you'd be serving."

Joanna smiled. "That would be after the class. However, if you're my only student, I could make an exception."

Before Lisa could respond, Eric and Helen's pickup came down the gravel drive.

Lisa laughed. "Guess I'll have to wait for the tea."

Minutes later, a car pulled in with California plates. The female driver practically jumped out of the car. Joanna walked up but didn't get a chance to introduce herself, as the woman immediately started speaking.

"As soon as I saw the flyer, I dropped my husband and kids off to wander the town. The flyer didn't say what style you'd be teaching, though."

"It'll be the Yang style," Joanna responded. "Do you practice?"

"Oh, yes—Wu, three days a week for two years. Have you been teaching long?"

Joanna smiled. "Thirty years, but always a student."

The woman slapped her forehead. "I'm sorry, I'm Maggie Styles. I'm just coming down from being cooped up with four boys. Well, the boys and my husband. Do you have a place where I can meditate?"

Joanna nodded. "Just around the side of the building, there's a little square of grass and a great view of the ocean."

Two unknown cars rolled in while she was talking with Maggie, but it looked like Helen and Lisa knew the drivers.

"Joanna, come over here." Lisa said. "I'd like to introduce you to Bobby Alvarez, the best part of the city council." Lisa looked around. "And Cheryl Chin is around here somewhere."

Helen winked at Joanna. "I think she went into the apothecary."

With a tight stomach, worried that Cheryl would find a dusty corner that she had missed, Joanna entered the front, where the herbs were displayed. From the corner of her eye, she saw a shadow move, cast from the light she'd placed over the shrine she had cleaned.

"Cheryl?"

The diminutive figure that was Cheryl stepped back from the shrine. "Yes, that's me."

"I just wanted to welcome you and thank you for the late-night soup."

"You were a pleasant late-night surprise," she said and looked back the way she'd come. "You've done a wonderful job creating this Shinto shrine."

"Thank you, but it was already here. All I did was dust it off and replace some of the incense."

Cheryl gave a short bow. "Beautiful nonetheless."

The two walked around to the side of the building, and Joanna gently touched Maggie, who was sitting zazen, on the shoulder. "Would you like to try Yang style?"

Maggie nodded and rose, following Joanna to a shaded area that was level but off the gravel, where the other students—seven in all—were assembled. The introduction was short, and Joanna explained that tai chi was considered a moving meditation that flexed every muscle and joint in the body. She demonstrated the first thirteen forms, facing north, then south. Then it began. Moving from student to student, she helped them with balancing, rolling the ball, hands float like clouds, and finally, grasping bird's tail, over and over. After half an hour, she introduced the beginning qigong form Swimming Dragon, then bowed to the class and invited them to tea.

Cheryl had to rush back to the Outpouring and Maggie begged off, saying that she had to go find her four boys, but everyone else stayed for the tea session.

Joanna was thrilled with the turnout and made sure that everyone walked away with a favorite tea. But one car remained. She looked around and couldn't find the owner, so she walked into the apothecary.

"Oh, Ms. Alvarez. Would you like me to show you around?"

"Yes, I'd love a tour. You know, from what I've seen, everything is so varied and evocative and powerful. You've done a wonderful job bringing the apothecary to life."

Joanna walked her to the back living area, where they discussed how simply these two doctors of Chinese medicine had lived. Next, they moved to the backroom, which was stacked high with boxes of herbs. When they came to the shrine, both women grew quiet. Finally, Joanna took Bobby to the herb shop. "This is where the Chinese community could come and shop for healing herbs and herb teas. It was from these herbs that prescriptions were filled. And that ends the tour," she concluded.

Bobby turned to face her. "That was wonderful, Joanna. I understand that you've had a rough time of it since you arrived in Dungeness Bay. I'd like to change that. How would you feel about making a presentation about the apothecary to the city council?"

"I'd love that, though I'll need some time to put something together."

"I'll propose the presentation to the other members and get back to you. Would a week be enough advance notice?"

"I can make that work."

She was surprised that as soon as Bobby drove off, Alex came up from the side of the building where the trail led to the beach.

"Judging from the wet pant legs, I'd say you've been wading in tide pools."

"That and chasing Rusty. I snuck out with him when you guys were having tea. The good news is that I'm feeling like my old self."

Joanna grinned. "I've got some good news myself."

Alex raised his eyebrows. "It's about time."

"I gave my first tour to Bobby Alvarez from the city council, and she wants me to put together a presentation for the board members."

Alex took a quick step, pulled her into a tight embrace, and whispered in her ear, "That's great."

Joanna didn't break away. Instead, she soaked up his scent and took in the feel of his body against hers.

Chapter Twenty-four

Joanna enjoyed Alex's full embrace, wondering if it was going to involve a kiss. For a minute, she felt like a schoolgirl once again, after her first date, when the boy walked her to the door. But there was no kiss, and it was just as well. Between the tai chi class, her upcoming presentation for the city council, and trying to figure out who killed Gus, she didn't feel she had the time or the energy for romance.

She and Alex did a walk through the apothecary with dust cloths and spray cleaners. After a while, he begged off to go upstairs and fix lunch. When he was gone, Joanna walked into the back room, where the dumbwaiter had crashed through its landing platform, depositing her and the ottoman in the basement. She slid the table to one side, exposing the narrow stone steps, and looked around for Rusty, who was sniffing at a box of herbs on one of the low shelves.

"Rusty, come here." He ran to her side. "Let's go down to the basement."

At the bottom of the steps, Joanna watched him for a reaction. "Do you see anything I should know about, like ghosts?"

She cursed herself for coming down without a flashlight. Still, with the light coming down the lift shaft and the stairs, it wasn't pitch black, but dark enough that she didn't want to venture into the room. Rusty was at her side, his head moving back and forth like someone watching a tennis match. When he stopped, he appeared to be staring at something to her left. She followed his gaze to see Doc Hay's figure.

"Hello. I am happy to see that you weren't hurt by your fall down the shaft the other day."

"Doc Hay?"

"Yes."

"Do you live down here? Oh, sorry, I mean—"

"I know what you mean. I'm able to move around the apothecary and the apartment upstairs. If I leave, it may only be to travel to the old smokehouse and root cellar."

"Was it you that told me to get out of my truck during the storm?"

"Yes."

"You had some special insight into the future?"

"No, I simply saw that the poplar that crushed your vehicle was swaying more than the other trees, and if it fell you would probably be killed." Doc Hay continued, "I like your friend. He is a nice man with good intentions."

"What? Do you mean Alex? How would you know something like that?"

"I can see intent through fields and colors of energy. The woman who occupied the apartment before you only had concern for herself. I believe she was a scribe assembling the story of Dungeness Bay. One day, her aura changed. I'd seen it before in another. I believe it has to do with greed.

"I never learned to read English, though I can speak it. Many a night I leaned over her shoulder as she worked her typewriter, trying to make out the words. I was only able to make out three: miners, sick, and gold. It was on her last day that her aura changed to a solid color, and I believe it was over the concern for the miners' gold."

"Wait, wait. You said that happened on her last day?"

"Yes. She'd been walking along the beach. I watched her come up the trail, walk past the cemetery and the apothecary to the smokehouse, where her energy flow ebbed to nothing. Concerned, and after some internal conflict, I decided that I should check on her, but she was gone."

"What do you mean, 'gone'?"

"She wasn't in the smokehouse, and she didn't return. Energy leaves a trail in the air, kind of like dust. She never returned, and there was no trail. She was simply gone."

"Joanna?" Alex's voice called out.

A light shone at her feet, and Rusty, who had been unmoving, was suddenly animated. He ran up the stairs, barked once, then ran down and barked at Joanna.

"Yes, Alex?"

"Lunch is ready. Are you alone? I thought I heard you talking with someone."

She quickly scanned all the shadows for Doc Hay, but he was gone.

Still processing the fact that she had just spoken with a ghost, she made her way up the narrow steps.

"I was just talking with Rusty," she lied. She didn't think any good would come from telling people she was talking to the ghost of the owner of the apothecary. "The lift crashed through its landing into this basement. What's for lunch?"

Alex shined the light down the steps, then turned to her and smiled. "Scallops and asparagus on a bed of rice."

Impressed, Joanna asked as she ascended the steps, "Oh my God, where did you learn to cook?"

Back in the apartment, the little kitchen table was already set. "What can I do?" Joanna asked.

"Sit. I'm doing lunch. You're up for dinner."

He waited on her, dishing the food onto her plate, then poured a glass of wine.

"Really, this is just my way of saying thank you. You pulled my fat out of the fire twice. Once when you let me recuperate in your spare bedroom and then again when you found me collapsed at my rental," he said and held up his glass of wine. "So, thank you."

Right then and there, Joanna wanted to run around the table and kiss him but decided a toast was perhaps more appropriate. She raised her glass.

"To the man who rescued my luggage in the pouring rain,

provided transportation—though the Ural still scars me and I still want a car—and helped me clean the apothecary. To friends."

They clinked glasses, and she thought she saw just a slip of disappointment on Alex's face at the word friends. To get through her awkwardness, Joanna commented on the meal and asked where he got the scallops.

Alex stood in response.

"Please sit. There's something I need to discuss with you," Joanna said.

"Sure thing," Alex said. "More wine?"

"You may want a lot more before I'm done."

He filled their glasses, draining the bottle.

"Alex, I think Thayer Spelling was murdered."

"What?" Alex sputtered.

"I'm pretty sure I know where the body is."

"What? How?"

Alex gulped down his wine and stood, ignoring the dishes on the table. He walked around and took Joanna's hand. "Let's go into the living room and discuss this."

She followed him, allowing herself to be directed. "Now sit."

Chapter Twenty-five

Alex pulled a chair around so he could face Joanna on the couch.

"Have you heard anything from the district attorney's office?" Joanna asked.

Alex held a hand up. "Have you got any kind of proof that you didn't kill Gus? Maybe an alibi?"

"I believe I was on the road headed up the one-oh-one when he was killed."

"When you got here, what was the first thing you did?"

"I arrived early and decided to check out the museum; you know, the apothecary."

"Right. That's when the tree crushed your truck."

"I had just gotten out when the tree fell."

"You were out of the truck when the tree hit it. Why did you get out?"

Joanna's ears burned, and eyes filled with tears, knowing he wasn't going to believe her answer and afraid that she would lose her only advocate.

"Alex..."

He reached over and took her hands in his. "You can tell me anything."

"I wasn't alone in the basement when you called me to lunch. I was speaking with Doc Hay."

"You're serious?"

"I pulled into the parking lot the night I arrived. The wind was battering the truck. A voice told me to get out of the truck, but no one was there."

Alex stared at Joanna, dumbfounded. "You're really telling me this ghost exists?"

"The day the dumbwaiter crashed through the landing, I was

inside trying to load the ottoman. That's when I was first able to see him."

He released her hands and sat back in his chair. "A ghost warned you that the tree was going to fall. Then he helped you when you crashed down into the basement."

"No, it was Rusty who counterbalanced some of the boards and pulled the weight off my legs."

"You never really gave me the details."

"I hardly believed it myself. I only just found out that it was Doc Hay's voice that I heard that night, saving my life."

"If you went to trial for the murder of Gus, what you just told me would make a great insanity plea. And you're also telling me that you think Spelling was killed and you know where the body is? This is crazy."

Joanna sagged into the couch; her voice had lost its energy. "It was during my conversation with Doc Hay that I learned of her death and the location of her body. He didn't tell me in so many words, but it wasn't hard to figure out from what he was saying."

Alex rocked forward, then back. "Joanna, I believe you. I do. But is there any way that this ghost, Doc Hay, can materialize or make himself known to me?"

"Tell Alex to place a coin on the desk," Doc Hay said, appearing suddenly.

Joanna's eyes went wide at the sound of Doc Hay's voice.

"Yes," she told Alex. "Place a coin on the desk."

"What? Why?"

"Doc Hay just told me to tell you to put a coin on the desk. Just do it."

Alex dug into his pocket, pulled out a quarter, and placed it on the desk.

"If I gather all my emotions—anger, fear, hate—and direct them at the coin, I believe that I can move it," Doc Hay said.

Joanna related to Alex, "Doc says he's going to move the coin."

Alex leaned forward, staring down at the quarter.

"Tell your friend to move away from the desk," Doc Hay directed.

"Alex, get away from the desk."

When he did, almost on cue, the quarter rose two feet above the desk and hovered, then it sailed across the room, embedding itself into the front door.

Alex staggered to the door, looking at Joanna. "Is it all right to pull it out?"

"Yes, I think so."

He pulled the quarter out and turned it over, examining both sides. Then, he tossed it in the air and watched it fall to the floor.

"Is your ghost here? Can Doc Hay hear me?"

Doc Hay said, "Tell him I can hear him but for some reason, I can't make myself visible to him."

Joanna relayed the information to Alex, who said, "Joanna, Doc, I believe, but I'll freak out another day. Right now, knowing where Thayer Spelling is buried is not only going to be something you can't explain but will further implicate you."

"There was a shrewd judge who lived during the Tang dynasty. I read many of his cases. Perhaps I can help," Doc Hay offered.

"Doc Hay wants to help. He says he's read many criminal cases solved by a judge in the Tang dynasty."

Alex ran his fingers through his hair. "We could use all the help we can get."

Joanna leaned back in the chair and stared up at the ceiling, where the image of Doc Hay was hovering.

"I believe that the dead man under the tree had something to do with the death of the scribe and that he was killed by an evil person who conspired with him to kill the scribe. Find the evil person and you will solve both murders."

"All right, this is driving me crazy," Alex said. "Joanna, you have to give me a sign that Doc Hay is talking to you so that I know that you're not staring at the ceiling because you're stroking out."

"Sorry. Doc thinks that Gus had something to do with Thayer's death and was conspiring with someone who, for some reason, killed him. What do you think?"

"I think it's a theory and a stretch, but right now it's better than anything I can come up with, which is nothing. Let's start with where you think Thayer's body is buried."

"I believe her body is either in the root cellar or in the smokehouse," Joanna said. For a minute, she looked puzzled. "During the storm, I took refuge in the smokehouse, so I guess that means that her body is in the root cellar."

Alex got up and walked into the kitchen. Joanna followed him in, trailed by Rusty.

"What are you doing?"

"Clearing the table and thinking," he said, placing the plates in the sink. "If you check the root cellar and find her body, I'll feel compelled to contact the sheriff, who is now Chuck Cowdrey. My guess is he'll wonder how we knew where to look. Does Doc have any idea who killed Gus, and does he know for sure that Gus killed Thayer?"

Doc Hay shook his head. "Please tell him I have told you all I know, and my theory. I have nothing to add at this time."

"Doc told us everything he knows. I think at this point, I need to put together a list of suspects. Sheriff Collins said that greed was the mastermind. This leads me to the conclusion that all these murders have something to do with the gold the miners paid Doc Hay and his partner for their services."

Chapter Twenty-six

"Wait. If that gold was never assayed or deposited, surely Doc Hay would know what happened to it."

"Tell Alex that my partner Long On was the bookkeeper and handled all the money. We felt it best that I did not know where the gold was hidden in the event I was arrested. I was the one who called upon patients at their homes, and so more likely to run afoul of the anti-Chinese cowboys who roamed the land."

Joanna made a face and looked over at Alex. "Doc has no idea where the gold is buried, but somebody thought that Thayer spelling did, and they killed her for that information."

Alex shook his head. "I don't think that whoever is behind the murders knows where the gold is but thinks it might be in the apothecary and that's why they've been sending you all those notes." He glanced at his watch. "I need to get up to Portland. It'll just be a couple of hours; I should be back in time for a late dinner. You okay with that?"

She looked at Alex with a puzzled expression. "Sure, but what's up in Portland?"

"Business."

"While you're gone, I'm going to put together a list of suspects. Maybe you can go over them with me when you get back?"

"Sure thing. Keep Rusty with you, and don't lean on any handrails."

They both laughed and did the dishes, then Alex disappeared into his room. Minutes later, wearing his leather jacket and jeans, he climbed in his taxi and drove off.

Joanna stood at the top of the stairs for a couple of minutes, wondering what business Alex could have in Portland. She shook off the question as something that was none of her business. After all, he was just a renter.

Joanna smiled. Perhaps that last embrace had taken him beyond being *just* a renter.

She stepped back into her apartment, closed the door and walked into her bedroom, where she pulled her journal out from under the mattress.

Dear Journal,

Alex and I embraced, and I felt something taking me back to those first days when K. C. and I were dating. There was no kiss—maybe next time. I just don't want to come across as too forward. I don't know what I'd do if he wanted to have sex. There is so much going on in my life. There just doesn't seem to be time for that. It seems that there's a lot I don't know about Alex. He's friendly and seems eager to please, and I know what people have told me about his background, but we've never had a heart-to-heart. Maybe, like the kiss, it's down the road.

I can't believe that I've been talking to a ghost. I've never believed in things that go bump in the night. Usually, they've been just that—things. He can move around my apartment and the apothecary and outside to the stone smokehouse.

I can see and hear him, and I think Rusty can too, but not Alex. When he was alive, the locals called him Doc Hay, though his real name is Ing Hay, and his partner was Long On. I wonder why he's a ghost but not his partner. At least, there's no sign of his partner, anyway. He explained that people carry an aura and leave a trail of energy. It was his voice the day I arrived that told me to get out of the truck. He explained it away as simply noticing that the tree that crushed my truck was swaying in the wind more than the others. He did mention that Alex was a nice guy with the right intentions, whatever that means, and that he could see this from his aura. Other than all this, he has no special insights into the murders.

Sheriff Collins said that greed is the mastermind of the murders. I take that to mean that whoever killed Gus and Thayer committed the murders because of the miners' gold that's supposed to be buried somewhere around the apothecary. Anyway, I've created a list of suspects consisting of Chuck Cowdrey, Mayor Calvin Ritter, and Alex's two friends, William Snow and John. I'd like to think that they really did come up from California to visit Alex while he was in the hospital in a coma, but who knows? Alex apparently has money, as evidenced by the three rentals, so I've taken him off my suspect list. The city council—Bobby Alvarez,— seems neutral. Lisa Posey, the owner of the Chocolate Factory, is hard to read. After my tai chi class, I found Cheryl Chin wandering around the apothecary so I'm going to add her to my suspect list. Eric and Helen Ward seem innocent enough and came up to help me set up for the class, though Eric wandered the apothecary with that screwdriver, staring at boards and beams, supposedly looking for dry rot. When I asked Helen what he was doing, she was quick to explain. I think I'll put them on my suspect list, too.

Joanna didn't want to be outdone by Alex's noontime meal of scallops and asparagus on rice but wanted some comfort food, so she fixed grilled sea bass with a side of pesto pasta and broccoli drizzled with butter.

As she set the table, the food staying warm on the stove, she wondered how late a late dinner was to Alex. She glanced at the clock on the wall but was distracted by the sound of tires on gravel and a horn honking.

"What now?"

She walked out to the landing and scratched Rusty between the ears. "It's someone in a black pickup," she murmured.

The driver didn't get out, which raised Joanna's suspicions.

"Come on Rusty, stay close."

Joanna stopped at the bottom of the stairs. It was an old, black Chevy Silverado. It looked like K. C.'s old Chevy.

Chapter Twenty-seven

Alex climbed out of the truck with a big grin. "What do you think?"

Joanna slowly circled the truck. "Where'd you get it?"

"Portland." He walked over and took her hand in his, turning it palm up and dropping the keys in her hand.

"It's the 2000 model, just like the one you were driving that got crushed by the tree."

Joanna's emotions hit her all at once, and she buried her face in his shoulder and began to cry.

"How did you do this?"

"It was easy. I contacted some veterans in Portland, told them what I was looking for." He held out a hand, indicating the truck. "And here it is."

"That's not what I meant," she said, stepping away and leaning on the truck. "You're just supposed to be a friend, a renter—you know, a helpmate."

Alex knelt down and ruffled Rusty's fur. "I don't think this takes me out of any of those categories."

Joanna stepped forward and took his hand. "Come on, dinner is getting cold, and I've got a list of suspects I want you to look at." Then she smiled. "Maybe, that is, after we take my truck out for a drive."

After dinner, the two walked onto the landing at the top of the stairs, sipping wine and leaning on the rail.

"I'd really like to pay you for the truck," Joanna began.

"Not a chance," Alex replied. "Then it wouldn't be a gift."

She turned to face him and placed a hand on his arm. "I'm confused."

"What, you're afraid that it's a gift with an ulterior motive?" He looked down at the truck for a moment. "Yeah, I guess in a way it is." Then he looked back at her. "But there are no strings. Joanna,

I like you because I like you. As for the truck, it makes you happy and that makes me happy. You have transportation that doesn't scare you, and I don't have to cart you back and forth to town. It's kind of a win-win."

She leaned in and kissed him on the lips, then stepped back and smiled. "Like how a kiss makes me happy and I hope makes you happy." She laughed. "Kind of a win-win. Oh yeah, and no strings attached."

They both laughed and walked down to the truck, Rusty at their heels. Joanna opened the door and checked the miles, and they took turns singing the virtues of having a pickup truck.

They didn't end up going for that drive. Instead, they went upstairs, refilled their wine glasses, and settled onto the couch with pencil and paper, listing suspects and looking for means, motive, and opportunity.

Joanna pointed at a name on the list. "I think we should start with Chuck Cowdrey. He became angry after listening in on a conversation I had with Thayer Spelling's editor at Beach Front Publishing."

"How so?" Alex asked.

"He said he had every right to eavesdrop. That was after telling me I could use his phone and that he didn't agree with Sheriff Collins about my guilt. He actually pulled his gun when Rusty growled at him."

"Wow," Alex said. "I know that he inherited a small amount of money when his father died. When the city hired him, he was promised housing, and they stuck him in that dump of a bungalow. But I also know that the sheriff confided in him. I think we need to talk to the previous sheriff and find out what he knows about the miners' gold because that will tell us what Cowdrey knows. Who else is on the list?"

"You might not agree, but I put the mayor on the list. I think it was Lisa Posey who said he had political ambitions. Finding the gold would certainly finance a political run for any office."

"I don't know. He was the one who saved the apothecary from being torn down. He got most of the local businesses behind him with the idea of turning the building into a museum—you know, more money into the coffers—but only some of the residents agreed. He seems to be a straight arrow with the best interests of the town at heart. Anyone from the town council make your list, though?"

"No, but I included Eric and Helen Ward."

"You're joking. Didn't they help you set up for your first class? Besides, they own the hardware store."

"Yeah, but Eric walked around the apothecary with a screw-driver, jabbing at the planks and beams, and when I asked Helen what he was doing, she jumped to his defense about having been a home inspector and that he was looking for dry rot. It looked to me like he was just wandering around."

"What about the Johnson woman who owns the Book Nook?" Alex wondered. "For someone who owns a bookstore, she seems standoffish. You know, I know a lot of the townspeople and most of the business owners, but I don't even know her first name."

"It's Louis. Collins asked if I wanted her to sit in while he was asking me questions. I'll put her on my list. I've also included Cheryl Chin from the Outpouring since she was wandering around the apothecary after the class."

Alex laughed. "You can't put everyone who wanders around looking at the apothecary on your suspect list. How do you plan on narrowing down the list?"

Joanna picked up the paper with the names of her suspects and stood. "Follow me." She led him to her room, where there was a whiteboard the size of a small school chalkboard nailed to her wall.

Joanna detailed her approach. "First, I'll put down the names, then, next to each name, the motive, means, and opportunity. Those who have all three will remain, while those that have only two—say, means and motive but no opportunity—will go to the bottom of the list. I'm going to start with a call to Collins."

Chapter Twenty-eight

Alex eyed Joanna. "So, you're going to interview each suspect?"

"No, I don't think that will work. But it's a small town, and Lisa Posey seems to know a lot. She knew where you used to live."

"It all looks good. I've got to go down to Crescent City, but I'll be back in a couple of days, and we can follow up on some of your suspects."

While you're gone I'm going to repair the Dumbwaiter shaft.

....

When Joanna arrived at the hardware store, she rolled the windows down and left Rusty in the cab, then pulled out her shopping list, looking it over as she pushed through the double doors. When she looked up, it was into the face of Eric Ward.

"Looks like you've got a list going. Can I help you find anything?"

"I'm changing the lock on the apartment. I'll also need a sheet of half-inch plywood cut to forty-eight by forty-eight inches, a handheld floodlight, a bag of three-quarter-inch wood screws, and fifty feet of stout rope."

"If you're changing the lock, you'll need a new doorknob," Eric commented. She followed him past three aisles and down a fourth.

Joanna pointed. "I need one of these brushed nickel."

She watched as he chose a hanging one that looked like it had been opened.

"Someone bought this and returned it. They opened it but everything is there. I haven't got a floodlight that's handheld, but I've got a flashlight almost as bright."

"That'll do."

She followed Eric back out to the front of the store to a display. "How about this one?" Eric offered. "It comes with a battery."

"Great, but I don't see any plywood."

"It's out back. You'll have to buy the four-by-eight-foot sheet, but I'll cut it down. You said forty-eight square inches?"

Joanna nodded.

"The screws are at the end cap of aisle five, right next to the coils of rope. Go ahead and get what you need. I'll cut the plywood and meet you at the register."

Joanna turned the flashlight on and off a couple of times, satisfied that it was bright, even in natural light. When she set it next to the register, she looked up from an odd sound and saw Eric sliding her plywood sheet along the floor.

At Joanna's look, he explained, "No reason to carry it if I don't have to." He rang up each item, then said, "Comes to forty-five dollars."

Joanna pulled out some folded bills from a front pocket and sorted out two twenties and a five.

"Oh, I never asked—did you find any dry rot?"

Eric's expression went blank, and he blinked. "You mean the other day. No, no dry rot at all."

"Helen said you used to be a home inspector. Was that here on the coast?"

"Ah, sure. I worked for Bay County. If you get the door, I'll carry this out for you."

After everything was loaded, Joanna bid Eric farewell. Driving back to her apartment, she went over her conversation with him. It seemed that he was coming up with answers on the spot rather than simply remembering. On a strange hunch, she drove over to Alex's vacant rental, found the key under a flowerpot, went in, and headed for the phone.

After hanging up, she thought about her conversation with the county clerk. She wasn't totally surprised when the county checked their records going back fifteen years and found no record of an Eric Ward ever working for the county.

She looked down at Rusty. "It looks like Eric and Helen belong on my suspect list."

When she returned to the truck, she rummaged around in the bag that contained the doorknob and discovered it only had one key. She tossed the bag on top of the rope that lay on the floor of the cab so that Rusty could stretch out.

Back at her apartment, she found that installing the doorknob was a snap. Then came the hard part—hanging the rope that pulled up the lift and replacing the landing.

Going back and forth from the apartment to the back room of the apothecary where the dumbwaiter's car poked up out of the floor, Joanna was able to loop the rope over the pulley and raise the little four-by-four car just above the splintered landing. She locked the rope in place so the car hung in its shaft just above the now open space. She cleared away damaged wood and slid the new sheet of plywood in place, then ran back upstairs and lowered the car on top. When the car and landing aligned, she ran back upstairs, noticing that Rusty didn't follow after the second trip up. She raised the car and locked it in place, then ran down and fastened the landing board in place with six screws on each side. Then, she lowered the car down one last time to make sure everything lined up.

"All right big guy, time to explore the basement and have a talk with Doc Hay."

Rusty waited patiently as Joanna retrieved the flashlight from the truck. He followed her as she made her way to the room with the small table with the lamp perched on top. Bending down, she grabbed one of the table legs and pulled, sliding a portion of the floor out almost three feet, revealing the steep, narrow stone steps. She turned on the flashlight and descended.

With the dumbwaiter landing in place, the only light aside from her flashlight came down the stairs.

"Doc Hay, are you here?" she called out, then looked down at Rusty. He was still as a statue, focused on the far corner of the room.

Chapter Twenty-nine

Hovering just above the floor was Doc Hay. She hadn't noticed his long queue and realized that she was seeing him in greater detail than before. Though his happi coat was black, she could now see large gold characters over the chest, but the rest of the material was printed in a series of circles filled with white blossoms. The bottom of the coat was hemmed in three-inch white trim that matched the trim at the end of each sleeve and the edges of the coat. One side connected to the other with frogs.

"I am here."

After taking a quick glance at Rusty, who was now stretched out on the floor, she asked, "Is there anything more you can tell me about the scribe?"

"Other than the change of color of her aura and that her energy trail had abruptly ended, no."

Rusty barked once and got up, brushing Joanna's leg. A moment later, her flashlight became the only source of light in the room. Rusty had moved to the foot of the steps. Someone had slid the little table with the lamp back in place.

"Doc?"

"Still here."

She ran up the narrow stone steps and pushed on the floor, unable to move it. There was nothing to hold on to that would allow her to slide that section of the floor.

She came back down, walked over to the new landing she'd installed for the dumbwaiter, and shined her light on the affair. She cursed, remembering that she had fastened it into place from above and then lowered the little car on top.

"We're sealed in," she told Rusty and Doc Hay.

Joanna sat down cross-legged and wondered how long the flashlight battery would last. As she sat, Rusty moved around the room, sniffing at everything.

"You might be interested to know," Doc Hay said, "that Long On and I had a booming business."

"Please, Doc, I just need to think. Alex should be back tomorrow, maybe the next day. He'll see the truck," she said and shined the flashlight on the ceiling. "The walls are stone, but the ceiling is plank. He's bound to notice that the apothecary is open and when he comes in, I'll hear him and pound on the ceiling."

Doc Hay continued. "As I was saying, the two of us had a booming business consisting of miners, locals, and sometimes folk from the timber industry. But as I had mentioned to you before, this basement was originally an opium den. As you can imagine, we couldn't have people coming to the apothecary who weren't sick. We needed a way to get them in and out of here, as well as an escape, in the event that some of the anti-Chinese factions tried to burn us out."

Joanna barely took in a word. Her mind was racing with questions. How long could she and Rusty go without water? She kept shining her light around the room, hoping to find anything that she could use to pound on the ceiling when Alex arrived.

"Rusty. Rusty, what are you doing?"

Joanna walked over to where he was digging around a series of five planks that ran from the floor to the ceiling.

"Is something there?" she asked him, shining the light at the floor where he'd been digging. "What is it?"

The image of Doc Hay floated down next to Rusty, who ignored the ghost.

"He's digging at the door to our escape tunnel, our way of smuggling our opium clients in and out."

"What are you talking about?"

"The tunnel that leads to the root cellar, as I tried to tell you earlier," Doc Hay responded.

Joanna placed the flashlight on the floor so that it shined on the portion of the planks where they entered the dirt floor. She pulled out her pocket knife and began stabbing the dirt, then digging. Rusty moved to the farthest plank and continued his own digging.

Struck with an idea, Joanna stood and removed her belt, then cut the four-inch by two-and-a-half-inch metal buckle from her leather belt. She knelt down and began to dig at the dirt she'd loosened with the knife.

Once the first plank was freed, she was able to pull out the remaining four. With bleeding fingers, she moved over and hugged Rusty around the neck. "This is going to get you an extra helping of kibble." Reaching down, she pulled up his front paws one at a time and examined each with the flashlight. "We're going to have to do something about those pads."

"All right Doc, you're telling me this tunnel leads to the root cellar?"

"That's correct. We installed these planks around 1915 but didn't bother blocking the root cellar."

"That's all I need to know. Come on Rusty, let's get out of here. Doc, I'll see you up in the apartment."

"I'll be waiting."

She watched his image vanish into the far stone wall.

"Come on Rusty."

The tunnel was oval, narrow, and just four feet high. Crouching and leading with the powerful light, Joanna slowly felt her way through the tunnel, dodging roots and, twice, having to crawl under a root the size of her thigh. Every few steps, she would turn off the light in hopes of seeing light at the end of the tunnel. When she did this for the tenth time, she was rewarded with a dim glow. The closer she got, the larger the glow, but it didn't grow brighter. She was soon confronted with ten stone steps that brought her up into a ten-foot by four-foot room lined with shelves, topped off with a high stone ceiling.

She turned sideways and moved across a plank floor to a

six-plank door that she was able to shoulder open. As soon as she was out of the building, she sat on the ground, called Rusty over, and hugged him close. But then she remembered that she, Alex, and Doc Hay had figured that the body of Thayer Spelling was in the root cellar. Either the three of them were wrong, or someone had moved the body. If that were the case, it was the same person who had murdered Gus or Thayer, or both, and had trapped Joanna in the basement.

Joanna pushed herself up and gently dabbed at her bloody fingertips with her shirttail while building up a head of steam. She marched down the trail and closed both apothecary doors, then looked at Rusty, who was by the stairs.

"Nope. Come on, big guy. We can clean up later. Right now, I have to confront Eric Ward."

She opened the passenger door. Rusty circled twice and made a running jump into the cab. As she walked around to the driver's side, Joanna slowed her pace and took calming breaths. She wanted to confront Eric with what she was sure he had done—shutting them in—but she didn't want to pound a confession out of the guy. After she climbed behind the wheel, she paused starting the truck.

Chapter Thirty

When Joanna pulled into the parking lot of the hardware store, rolled down the windows for Rusty and took a deep calming breath.

"Rusty, I want you to wait here," she said, stroking his back. "If you hear me call, you come a running."

Joanna pushed through the double doors of the hardware store and looked around, surprised when she saw Helen walking up an aisle to greet her, not Eric.

"Joanna, hi. Is there anything I can help you with?"

"I need to talk to Eric."

"I'm afraid that's not possible. Can I help you find something?"

"Where's Eric?"

Helen made a face. "He's had one of his dizzy spells. I found him on the floor and managed to get him into the back room on the cot there. I'm sure he'd be happy to talk to you, but he really shouldn't try to get up."

"I just need a moment with him."

Helen frowned. "All right. He's back here," she said, motioning with her head. "The town veterinarian, Stan, has helped him before, so I gave him a call. I think he's with him now."

Joanna stopped just inside the little room. The veterinarian was at the head of the cot, cradling Eric's head between his hands.

"Okay Eric, I want you to relax. I'm going to move your head to the right really quickly, at the count of three."

Joanna cringed as the vet snapped Eric's head to the right then slowly brought it to center and did it again.

"That should help."

Joanna stepped out of the room and tapped Helen on the arm. "What's wrong with him?"

"Apparently the tiny balls that reside in the inner ear get

dislodged. That's when he gets so dizzy, he can't stay on his feet. What the vet does with those quick motions is to lodge the balls so they stop tumbling around. Eric has been down for a while. He should be on his feet in a couple of hours."

Joanna turned to leave.

"What was it that you wanted to ask him?"

"It can wait." She pushed through the double doors and walked up to the truck.

"That your dog?"

She turned and was greeted by a giant of a man, at least six feet six inches with wide shoulders, muscular arms, and a full head of salt and pepper hair.

She smiled. "Helen said you're a veterinarian." She extended her hand. "I'm Joanna Bright and," she indicated to the open window, "this is Rusty."

"Stanley Horton," he said, and shook her hand. "Pleased to meet you." Then he turned to Rusty. "And pleased to meet you."

Rusty reached up a paw that Stanley took with good humor. He looked over at Joanna. "He has some abrasions on his pads. My office is on the next block. Why don't you follow me, and I'll take care of those paws."

It took Joanna just five minutes to pull into the small parking lot, next to Stan's SUV, in front of an old wood structure that looked no bigger than a two-car garage. She walked around and opened the passenger side door. Rusty jumped out and moved around to her side.

"That is one well-trained dog," Stan said, leaning on his SUV.

"He is that and much more." She laughed. "A male companion that just listens."

Joanna was suddenly embarrassed and realized that she felt slightly attracted to this handsome man.

"I'm sorry, I don't know where that came from."

"No doubt Rusty is a great listener. If you care to tell me how he abraded his pads like that, I assure you I too will be a good listener."

"I live above the apothecary," Joanna began, sighing "I'm the new caretaker."

"Of course—Joanna Bright. That's why your name sounded familiar. I was in the Chocolate Factory when I heard your name come up."

She and Rusty followed Stan into his office to a room just off a very short hall.

He patted a low-padded platform and Rusty jumped up. Stan stepped on a pedal, making the platform slowly rise. It stopped when Rusty, who had laid down, was chest-high.

Stan looked over to Joanna. "You were about to tell me about his paws."

She took a seat in the corner. "I managed to lock us in the basement, and we had to dig around some boards to get out."

"Ah." Stan nodded. "I noticed that your paws were also a little abraded too."

Joanna chuckled. "Won't he lick off whatever you apply?"

"It's designed to soak in rapidly. If you've got fifteen minutes, that's all it will take, then I can wash it off."

Stan began to palpate Rusty's body, feeling here, touching there, and peering into his ears. "Rusty is a really healthy dog, especially for his size."

"I'm glad to hear it. I kind of inherited him. What do I owe you?"

"I wish all my patients were this well-behaved. The first visit is on the house."

Stan lowered the platform and, with a cue from Joanna, Rusty leaped off and padded to her side. Stan led them down the hall, through the front office, and out into the parking lot.

"Aside from treating Eric, this is my day off. Would you let me buy you a cup of coffee? The Outpouring sound all right?" He laughed. "Either that or the bar."

Joanna liked the soft tones of his laughter and decided on the spot that she would like to know this man better.

Chapter Thirty-one

Joanna pulled around behind the Outpouring, the only place she could park. Moments later, she watched as a motorcycle pulled up next to her. There was only one spot left, which was at the very end of the lot. She hoped Stan would pull up next to her, and thought of asking the black-clad rider to move his motorcycle. But she changed her mind when he dismounted and removed his helmet; it was Stan.

Joanna attempted to hide her surprise, but it didn't work.

Stan hung his helmet on the motorcycle's sissy bar, walked over, and leaned on the pickup truck.

"Were you expecting me to drive up in a car with a magnetic sign on the side?"

"Maybe not a magnetic sign, but not on a motorcycle, either."

"When the weather permits, it's a cheap way to make house calls. The saddlebags can carry everything I need."

Joanna rolled down the windows and got out of the truck.

"You sure you want to have coffee with a biker?" Stan teased.

"Before I got this truck, I was riding a Ural."

Stan looked impressed. "That's cool. Now, why don't you find a booth while I'll get the coffee?"

Joanna smiled. "I take it black."

Fifteen minutes later, Stan came over to the booth Joanna had selected. He set down the two mugs of coffee, peeled off his leather jacket and tossed it onto his side of the booth, then slid in.

"Have you been here before?" Stan asked.

"Yeah, just the other night. Why?"

"Cheryl took my order and asked after you."

Joanna cocked her head. "What do you mean?"

"She wanted to know if it was you that I came in with."

"Really?"

"She knows I've got a partner—was probably wondering what I was up to."

She tried to hide her expression—this time disappointment—again but failed.

"Hey, I wasn't trying to mislead you by asking you to coffee. It just seemed like a friendly gesture."

"It is, and I thank you. You know, I have to ask. You're a pretty big guy. Did you play sports before becoming a veterinarian?"

"Nope. Despite what people think when they first meet me, I never played basketball or football. I was a contractor who built a few houses. I could see that it was going to take a toll on the body, so I changed careers."

"Honestly, I'm surprised you can survive as a vet in a town this size."

Stan shrugged. "I still do a little carpentry on the side."

"Do you know where the apothecary is?"

"I haven't been out there in years. It's on China Bluff, as I remember."

"I've been eyeing the space behind the building since I arrived. Would you be interested in building a deck for me? I'll pay top dollar for your time."

"I'd have to see what you have in mind—figure cost of materials and all."

"I'm heading back to my apartment from here. Do you have the time to take a look?"

"Sure," Stan responded. "As I said, this is my day off."

Stan followed her to the north edge of town, letting her pull ahead once they reached the gravel. She had pulled to the far left in the parking area next to four cars, not sure who was visiting or why, when she saw Bobby Alvarez.

Joanna let Rusty out of the cab and was met by Bobby, who looked past her to Stan, who was just getting off his motorcycle.

"I hope I'm not interrupting anything," Bobby said. "I proposed the idea of you doing a presentation for the city council and they all liked the idea but wanted to come out here and take a look around. I told them about the tour you had given me."

Stan walked up, helmet under his arm. "Joanna, I can come back another day if that would be better?"

"Not at all."

Joanna made the necessary introductions. "Bobby Alvarez, this is Stan Horton. I'm trying to talk him into building a deck behind the apothecary."

"Of course, the veterinarian. My husband brought in our cat."

"Give me just a minute to show Stan where I want the deck."

"Go on. I think the rest of the council would be interested to see what you have in mind for the grounds around the apothecary."

Stan was stepping out the dimensions of the deck when the council walked around the corner.

They formed a loose half-circle around her. "Joanna, this is Barry Caps, leader of the band," Bobby said, indicating the man next to her.

He smiled and gave a short bow. "Pleased to finally meet you. It was Jane's idea to greet you with dinner."

Jane stepped forward. "This would be a beautiful place for a deck. Would you be teaching tai chi on it?"

Joanna looked over at Stan. "If he approves the sight." Jane broke away from the group and walked to the center of where the deck would be as another man stepped forward with his hand outstretched.

"Hello there, Ms. Bright. I'm Dutch Barton. When Ms. Alvarez mentioned a presentation, I thought it would be a good idea to come out, and see if we could talk you into giving us a tour. Sorry about the weather when you arrived. None of us anticipated a storm."

Stan saved Joanna from responding when he walked up and touched her on the arm.

"Excuse me," she said and turned to face Stan.

"I could build you a thirty-by-fifty-foot deck. It would come close to the edge of the bluff, and I'd have to stabilize the ground a bit, and sink a couple of cement pillars. But it's doable."

"Let me know how much you need for supplies and how soon you can start."

When she turned back around, the council members were gone. She rounded the building and frowned. Both doors were open, and the council was nowhere to be found, though she heard voices.

She followed the voices and entered the apothecary to find the mayor holding up a bottle of a brown liquid.

"Mayor Ritter?"

He put the bottle back on the shelf and turned around. "Ms. Bright, I hope you don't mind. I have a key to the apothecary. When I got here, the council was just standing around, so I let them in."

Joanna was surprised that the mayor had let in the council members but reminded herself that the apothecary belonged to the city and that she was just a caretaker. But it still felt kind of odd.

She looked past the mayor to see a familiar face. "Helen?"

At the sound of her name being called, Mrs. Ward seemed to start. "I hope you don't mind. I came with mayor Ritter. I just couldn't resist getting an official tour."

"Not a problem. How's Eric?"

"He's up and about, still a little wobbly."

Councilmen Caps and Barton stopped tapping on the wall behind the shrine when they saw Joanna approach.

"Gentlemen, as soon as I can get you all together, I'll start the tour," Joanna said.

Caps turned. "I think Jane and Bobby are in the back room. I'd be happy to get them."

"You can join Helen and the mayor. I'll just be a minute," Joanna said.

After she gathered the council members, including the mayor and Helen, Joanna started the tour with an explanation of what the Chinese community was like when the apothecary was operating but had a distinct feeling that everyone was just being polite. Walking into the various rooms was like herding cats. Someone was always wandering off.

Frustrated, she led them past the living quarters, kitchen, stockroom, and out the back door, drawing their attention to the location of the deck Stan was going to build.

The council members came up one at a time to say good night until only the mayor and Helen remained.

Chapter Thirty-two

Helen, looking bored, said her goodbyes, and Mayor Ritter spoke briefly with Stan before departing.

"That was rather strange, don't you think?"

With a start, Joanna recognized the voice of Doc Hay and entered the apothecary through the back door. "Doc?"

"Here, in the living quarters."

She walked down the short hall. Doc Hay was hovering, almost like he was leaning against the back wall of the little living area. Joanna looked back down the hall before entering, to make sure Stan wasn't following her.

"What was strange?"

"Your friends were wandering around like so many children in a sweet shop, touching everything."

"Touching or looking for something."

Doc Hay's image began to shimmer. "One cannot see what is not there." Then he was gone.

"Hey," Joanna protested. "What's that supposed to mean?"

She was tempted to go down to the basement and confront Doc, but thought better of it. Instead, she turned and went to find Stan, who walked over when he saw her come out the back door.

"What did the mayor have to say?" she asked.

"I think he just wanted to know who was paying for the deck."

"Is this going to be a big job?"

"Not really. It's nothing I haven't done before, but it might take a while. I've got to work it into my schedule."

She hadn't gotten a note from the killer in a couple of days but decided to drop by the hardware store to see how Eric was doing and pick up a paddle lock for the front doors. Rusty was sleeping under the desk. She figured that with tender pads, the apartment was the best place for him.

At the hardware store, Eric, who had recovered, explained three times while they walked the aisles to a row of paddle locks, how awful it was to feel so dizzy.

"I'm so glad you're back on your feet," Joanna said. "Say hi to Helen for me."

Eric walked her to the door. When she drove out of the parking lot, she glanced into her rearview mirror. Eric was still watching her.

The last business at the south end of town was the Dungeness Bay Bar and Grill. Joanna was just hungry enough to be curious and pulled into one of five unoccupied parking slots.

Inside, the bar was darkly paneled, with a deep red bar backed by a long mirror, and a plank wood floor that reminded Joanna of the floor in her apartment. Her eyes smarted and she smelled something familiar that she couldn't quite put her finger on. There was no bartender and not one of the tables was occupied.

"Terry is in the back."

The voice came from a figure slumped over the far end of the bar. Joanna walked over and slid onto a stool. She glanced up at the chalkboard menu, then at the stranger.

"How's the food?"

"You smell the onions? That should tell you all you need to know. Chili's for lunch."

A man entered from the kitchen and asked, "Who are you talking to, Sam?" He looked up the bar at Joanna. "Sorry, I didn't hear you come in. What can I get you?"

Terry Chambers stood a solid six feet. He had a shaved head, a Roman nose with a slight bend, and cauliflower ears.

"Smells like chili and onions," Joanna observed.

"You've been talking to Sam."

"That, and I've got a nose."

He walked down the bar until he was across from her and extended his hand. "Terry Chambers."

She took his hand and gave it a squeeze. "Joanna Bright.

Boxing?"

He self-consciously ran a finger down his nose. "Judo."

She gauged his age to be about forty-five. "How far did you get?"

"World games, but not the Olympics. Did it for twenty-eight years. I'm retired now. I bought this bar and swore off breakfalls." Terry paused, then asked, "Does your husband play?"

She smiled. "No."

"You?" he said, his voice filled with surprise.

"I played a little in my youth but decided I like staying on my feet and went for a stand-up system."

He raised his eyebrows. "Tae Kwon Do?"

"Close combat—Chinese Kenpo."

He bobbed his head and gave her a wink. "How far did you get?"

She returned the wink. "Fifth black for thirty-three years before retiring to tai chi."

"Very pleased to meet you, Joanna Bright. You just passing through?"

"I'm the new caretaker of the old apothecary. I live upstairs."

"In that case, lunch is on the house," Terry said as he backed through the swinging door that led to the kitchen.

Joanna took a moment to look around, turning a circle on the barstool.

Sam held up his beer mug to get her attention, then slipped off his stool, sliding his mug along the bar as he approached Joanna. "Dungeness Bay Bar and Grill—a unique name, that."

"What?"

"The bar's name is as old as the structure. Well, except for the 'bar and grill' part. Terry added that when he bought the place."

Joanna nodded to be polite and tried to maintain eye contact.

"Built in 1888 and one hundred and thirty years old. Served the miners and a few of the lumberjacks."

Chapter Thirty-three

"Are you bothering Ms. Bright?"

Sam lifted his mug off the bar and returned to the far end. "Nothing of the sort. Just providing a history lesson," he grumbled.

Terry set a steaming bowl of chili on the bar, then grabbed a napkin and spoon and slid them across to Joanna. "What do you want to drink?"

"The lightest beer on tap."

Joanna lifted a spoonful of chili and held it just below her nose.

"If you can guess the ingredients, you eat free for a month."

"You're on," she said and made a show of tasting the chili. "Beans, tomatoes, and onions. No, wait. That would be a red onion." She took another spoonful. "Rich, dark brown sugar, but just a bit. Mexican chili powder, and for sure cumin. I taste just a pinch of cloves. On the back of my tongue is the bite of chipotle, then there's coriander."

"What about the meat?"

"You got me. I'm not much of a meat-eater."

Terry grinned. "Rattlesnake meat marinated for three days to modify the flavor but keep the texture. Sorry, you don't get to eat free for a month, but I'll give you a consolation prize of twenty percent off anything in the house, including alcohol." Terry glanced away as several people pushed through the entrance. "Ah, my people await. See you later Joanna?"

"Absolutely, and thanks for the chili."

After Joanna finished eating, she turned to face Sam. "Thanks for the history lesson."

He raised his mug in her direction. "Next time, I'll tell you a secret."

"Next time."

She walked out to the parking lot. For just a second, she wanted to go back and ask Sam to divulge that secret. But shook off the urge and started her truck, noticing that the gas gauge was just kissing empty.

The only gas station in Dungeness Bay was at the south end of town, Jupiter Discount Gas. When she pulled in, a young teen stepped out of the garage, wiping his hands on a cloth.

"You wanna fill it up?" he called out.

"As a matter of fact, I do. I think I've been running on fumes. Fill it with regular."

The teen walked toward her, eyeing the truck. "Two thousand Chevy. How many miles?"

"A little over two hundred thousand. Are you the mechanic here?"

He shook his head. "I just pump gas. That's my car in the garage. Something wrong with your truck?"

"No, but I live out all the way on China Bluff, and if I need a mechanic, I want to know where to go."

"China Bluff, right. The city hired you to take care of the old apothecary. Last I heard, the place was falling apart. The city was going to tear it down and turn the bluff into a park. The mayor stopped that with a bunch of signatures. But anyway, I'm a pretty handy guy. You got anything out there that needs fixing?"

Before Joanna respond, the gas pump clicked off and the kid kept talking. "You were running on fumes all right. It took twenty-four gallons. I think it only holds twenty-five. That's fifty-five dollars."

She gave him three twenties and followed him into the station's office.

"How are you with a hammer and saw?" Joanna questioned.

He handed her the change. "What do you need?"

"Do you know Stan Horton?"

"The veterinarian, sure."

"He's building a deck for me in between clients. I teach tai chi and would like the deck finished sooner than later."

"This gig is only part-time, so I could use the work, but like I said, my car is in the garage."

She stepped around him and looked at the orange car.

"Nice looking Karmann Ghia you got there. What's the problem?"

"Needs shocks. The originals are bleeding all over the place."

"Where do you get parts around here?"

"You don't. Lincoln City has an old salvage yard with what I need."

Joanna figured the kid for seventeen, maybe eighteen, and flashed back to when she and K. C. found out they couldn't have children. She had only been thirty-two. If she'd gotten pregnant, her son or daughter would be about this boy's age.

"How much for the shocks?"

"Two hundred for all four. Why?"

"I'll hire you for a week at twenty-five dollars a day, and pay you in advance—a check all right?"

The boy's eyes widened. "Yeah, great." He wiped his dirty right hand on his jeans and held it out. "Bud Nichols."

She shook his hand. "Joanna Bright. We have deal?"

"Yes ma'am, but it'll take a couple of days for UPS to bring them down and then another couple of days to install."

"When's your next day off?"

"I'm three days on four days off, and this is my third day."

"Good, I'll pick you up tomorrow at noon, right here."

Joanna drove away from the station, feeling that things were looking up. She'd made a new friend, hired someone to help Stan build her deck, and she had seven tai chi students. She went straight back to what she was finally beginning to think of as her apartment rather than just the apothecary.

When she got to the edge of the gravel parking area, she could hear Rusty barking.

"Oh boy. Rusty is probably desperate to get out."

She drove the remainder of the way onto the parking lot with a feeling of euphoria. When she got out of the truck, she was surprised to hear Rusty still barking. "That's odd," Joanna said out loud, tensing.

Rusty wasn't a barker. He must have sensed something.

Chapter Thirty-four

Joanna walked up the stairs, pulling the apartment key from her pocket.

The closer she got to the door the more frantic the barking grew. "Rusty, Rusty, it's okay."

When she opened the door, he ran past her and down the steps, faster than she'd ever seen him move. She closed the door and turned in time to watch Rusty run into the forest of poplar and red alder. Moments later, William Snow appeared, backpedaling out of the woods onto the parking area.

She ran down the stairs, stepped into a straddle position, and placed her hands on her hips.

"Rusty, come." He immediately ran to her side. "All right, what are you doing in my forest?" Joanna demanded.

"Alex will be in California a couple of days longer than planned and wanted me to hang around the apothecary. He said someone had been sending you threatening notes and even slit the brake line on the Ural."

Joanna pulled the gun from the holster in the middle of her back, then reached down and scratched Rusty between the ears. "Good boy. Between my Glock and Rusty, I'm feeling pretty safe."

"No new threats?"

"Not so far today. What are you doing camping in the woods?"

"I figured maybe I could surprise the culprit. After all, someone's delivering these notes."

"I set up some motion sensor lights and a camera where the driveway opens up to the parking area," Joanna told Snow. "I'm having pasta for dinner. Do you want to join me?"

"Sure, thanks."

Joanna looked around. "Where's your motorcycle?"

"I stashed it behind some trees just off the road."

"While I'm dishing up the pasta, bring down your bike and park it next to the Ural."

"I'll tell you what. You dish up real slow and I'll ride into the town deli and pick up some garlic bread."

"Deal. Grab a bottle of wine while you're at it."

As Joanna prepared dinner, Rusty stretched out at the entrance to the kitchen and watched her.

"We're having a guest for dinner, so no barking." Joanna wagged a finger at him.

At the sound of a motorcycle approaching, she walked to the kitchen window, surprised that it wasn't Snow. In fact, it was Stan. She walked out to the landing and shouted down.

"Stan, what's up?"

"I had a cancelation and figured I'd get a start on your deck."

"Sure thing. Are you hungry? I made pasta."

He pulled a toolbox out of his saddlebag. "I grabbed a bite in town."

Snow returned shortly thereafter and idled across the parking lot before parking next to the Ural. With a small bag, he walked up the stairs and knocked twice.

Joanna opened the door. "Come in. Rusty is a little restless. Aside from Alex, we haven't had much in the way of company."

Snow set the bag on the kitchen counter and pulled out a couple of cloves of garlic and a loaf of French bread.

"Where's the wine?"

"I stopped drinking years ago, so it slipped my mind. I noticed you've got company."

"What? Oh yeah, I've got the veterinarian building a deck for me. You saw his motorcycle?"

"Vet? Should I be confused?"

Joanna laughed. "Stan does carpentry on the side. He's fitting me in between clients."

Dinner was mostly filled with small talk.

"What's Alex up to?"

Snow forked a mouthful of pasta and kept his eyes on his plate.

Joanna looked at him, furrowing her brows. "Is there a problem?"

"You remember John?" Snow asked.

Joanna nodded.

"Well, he's a brawler. He got himself thrown in jail for a drunk and disorderly. Alex went down to bail him out." Snow paused. "I'm not supposed to be telling you this, but Alex may be bringing John back with him."

Joanna made a face. "This is going to get awkward. Alex has been renting a room from me."

They finished the garlic bread in silence. Snow carried his plate to the sink, then turned to Joanna. "I've got an idea."

"Shoot."

"John and I are builders. Maybe if your veterinarian doesn't mind, we could help him with the deck. Alex could continue to rent from you, and we could camp here."

Joanna nodded. "Sounds like a plan. Speaking of camping, you can stay in Alex's room until he returns."

"Thanks, but it wouldn't feel right. Besides, I've got my tent set up in the woods."

"Why don't you come down with me and we can talk to Stan?" Joanna asked. She walked to the counter, picked up a dishtowel, and threw it at Snow. "First things first. I'll wash, you dry."

After cleaning, they descended the steps with Rusty in the lead and walked around to the back of the apothecary where Stan was staking out the corners of the deck.

Joanna stepped around one of the stakes. "Am I standing on where the deck will be?"

"That's right about where I'm going to put the steps."

"Perfect. Stan, this is my friend William Snow."

"Just call me Bill," Snow offered.

She watched, pleased when the two men shook hands. "Would you mind if Bill and his friend John helped with the deck?"

"Fine with me. I know that you want your deck finished as soon as possible, and I'm booked back-to-back for at least two weeks."

"Any time you can squeeze in deck work, early or late is okay. You're still my main man. We'll get out of your way now," Joanna said. "Bill, show me your campsite."

When they had walked around to the front parking area, Bill stepped close. "The guy is gay," he said.

Joanna looked taken aback. "Really? How do you know?"

Bill ran a hand through his hair. "I just know."

"Does that bother you?"

"Hell no. John's gay. They're just people."

"Will John and Stan get along?"

"Are you and Alex having sex?" Bill suddenly blurted.

Joanna took a step back. "*What*?"

"Sorry," Bill apologized hastily. "My sense is that you and Alex are just friends, and that's all. I suspect that John and Stan will become friends as well. If their being gay bothers you, I can contact Alex and tell him not to bring John."

Joanna shook her head. "It doesn't bother me in the least. Now, where's your camp?"

They were twenty feet into the woods when they came to a grove of poplar trees intermingled with red alder, making a tall wall of sorts. Bill touched Joanna on the shoulder. "Stop and tell me what you see."

"A bunch of trees."

"Stay here."

Joanna watched him step between a poplar and red alder and vanish.

"Bill?"

"Step between the same trees I did," his voice directed.

When she did, she saw the walls of a canvas tent that were a vertical six feet and tapered down to just two feet.

Joanna reached out and touched one of the sides. "That's incredible. I wasn't ten feet away, and you just vanished."

"It's just a one-man tent, but the canvas blends in perfectly with the poplar," Bill said, smiling.

Chapter Thirty-five

Joanna rolled into the Jupiter gas station and found Bud leaning against his Karmann Ghia with a sad expression.

She parked next to him and slid out of the truck. "Why the long face?"

"Jake, the owner of the station, is letting me go."

"Okay, let's talk about it over lunch. I'm buying."

"You don't understand," Bud replied morosely.

"Then fill me in."

Bud looked like he was going to cry; he turned his back to Joanna.

"It can't be that bad," Joanna said reassuringly.

He turned to face her. "Yeah, it is. It's that bad. I've been sleeping in my Ghia. I'm homeless, and now I don't have any place to park."

She looked at the license plate. "Looks like the car's licensed."

"Yeah, and insured. I just made a payment. That gives me thirty days to get it off the street."

Joanna took a calming breath, which wasn't lost on Bud.

"This isn't your problem," Bud said.

"This isn't a problem, actually," Joanna replied.

"It's not a problem? I can't search for a job because I don't have transportation. This is a problem, and it's all mine. I won't be able to pay you back for a while."

"Does that mean that you can't help build my deck?"

"Everything I own is in that car. I need to find a place to store it first."

"Can you drive it up to China Bluff?"

"The apothecary? Yeah, but the shocks are bleeding out. Besides, do you really want a Karmann Ghia in your parking lot?"

Joanna gave him a look at the absurdity of that question and took another deep, calming breath.

"Why do you keep doing that?"

"It slows me down and keeps me centered and grounded."

Bud squinted at her. "Who the hell are you?"

"Your solution. Now follow me up to the apothecary and I'll show you where to park."

"No. I can't do this."

"You can and you will. We have a deal, and you're just bringing along some baggage."

He held up both hands like someone was holding a gun on him. "Thirty days, I pay you back, then I'm gone," he said, climbing in the VW and firing up the engine. He honked and gave her a thumb up.

When they reached the apothecary's parking lot, Joanna parked in front, got out, and waved Bud around to the side, where he parked next to the Ural. She noticed that Snow's motorcycle was gone.

She moved up to the side of the Ghia and looked inside for the first time.

"What's with the tanks?"

Bud climbed out and stood next to her. "I weld. Those are acetylene and oxygen. Uh, also, I have a confession."

Joanna was beginning to wonder what she'd gotten herself into with this young man. She had to figure out who killed Gus Hasselbacker and what happened to Thayer Spelling before the investigator for the district attorney arrived.

She pinched the bridge of her nose. "All right, fess up."

"I work with wood, but not building decks and big stuff."

"Come with me," Joanna sighed.

He followed her to the front of the apothecary, and Joanna opened the doors. "I've got shelves falling apart and plank floor that's splintering. If I get you the materials, can you keep this place from completely breaking down?"

Bud nodded. "I can do that."

"Good. You're on the clock. I want you to come up with a list of things you'll need," she said, and looked at her watch. "You've got two hours."

"What about my stuff?"

"Later. Two hours."

Then she walked out, leaving Bud in the apothecary, and went up to her apartment to let Rusty out and journal for a bit.

When she entered and Rusty uncurled from beneath the desk, she wondered how old he was and how much longer he'd be able to negotiate the steps.

She left the door open, knowing he'd return after doing his business and checking out Bud.

Dear Journal,

I have made some decisions that have both burdened and committed me and am feeling the ticking clock. Only four days until the DA's investigator shows up. Alex and I have put together a list of suspects, locals who would have an interest in the gold. Someone's got gold fever, I guess—something that would drive them to murder.

Joanna gazed across the room from the club chair, as was her habit when writing in her journal. She looked toward Rusty's usual spot under the desk, forgetting she had let him out.

"Your four-legged companion is with your hired hand."

"Doc Hay?"

"I suggest that you come down to the basement."

The shimmering image of the former owner of the apothecary flickered out then reappeared by Joanna's door. "Time for you to put down that journal and adjourn to the smokehouse. Before it's too late."

Doc Hay tilted his ghostly head. "I hear the alarm being sounded now," he said.

Joanna got up, dropping her journal on the chair, all the time trying to decipher what Doc Hay was talking about. She stepped out onto the platform at the top of the stairs and was greeted by a very agitated Rusty. He looked up at her and barked, then turned in a circle and urged her on with more barking.

"Okay, Rusty. All right," she said, picking up on his excitement and running down the stairs. "Let's go, let's go."

She raced down the trail to the smokehouse, arriving just after a still very agitated Rusty.

The old stone structure was split. The room where she'd huddled that first night had a false floor that could be lifted to reveal stone steps leading down to the root cellar and the tunnel that connected with the basement of the apothecary. On the other side of the building was a door that opened to the smokehouse. It had a plank floor.

Rusty led her around to the side of the smokehouse, where she found Bud sitting among a pile of floor planks, the shimmering image of Doc Hay hovering next to him. Both were staring down into the ashes.

She took in the sight of the ghost, dog, and Bud. "What?"

Bud stood and brushed off the seat of his pants. "I shouldn't be here."

Joanna stepped over some planks and looked down at the body of Thayer Spelling. "Oh, shit."

Chapter Thirty-six

Bud moved past her, stepping over and around the floor planks. "Bud, wait. I can explain."

"Right, you can explain why there's a body under a floor. Okay, I'm listening."

"I believe this is the body of Thayer Spelling."

"So, you knew her. All right, then you killed her."

"No, but I have to find out who did, or I'll be charged with a murder I didn't commit." Joanna put her hands up, trying to placate Bud. "Let's go back to my apartment and I'll explain."

"Explain what?"

Bud and Joanna looked toward the voice, down the trail where it came around the smokehouse, to the looming figure of William Snow.

Bud took a step forward. "Explain the body," he said, instantly regretting his words. "Who are you?"

"This is my friend, William Snow," Joanna said.

Snow walked past the two and looked down at the body in the ashes, then over at Joanna.

"Right. I want to hear this explanation too."

Joanna talked as she walked. "The last person to act as caretaker of the apothecary was a woman named Thayer Spelling, who vanished without a word."

"You're saying that's her in the ashes?" Snow asked.

"Get this," Bud blurted out. "The DA's sending someone down to arrest her for the murder of that woman."

"That true, Joanna?"

"It's complicated." Joanna grimaced.

"When's this DA guy coming down, and who's the kid?"

"Bud works for me, and they're not blaming me for her murder—not yet, anyway. Nobody knows about her body but us.

The district attorney thinks I killed Gus."

When they entered the apartment, Rusty curled up under the desk. Bud pulled out the desk chair, and Snow tossed Joanna's journal onto the couch and sat in the club chair. Joanna grabbed a pillow and sat in one corner of the couch with her legs crossed.

"First things first," Snow said. "What makes the DA think you killed Gus?"

"The last thing Sheriff Collins did before resigning was file a report filled with his suspicions about who killed Gus, which points at me. I found Gus's body the day I arrived. At first, he thought that Gus was blackmailing Alex, then I guess you and John set him straight. Collins figured that I had heard about the miners' gold and that Gus had been working with Thayer Spelling, who was putting clues together about the location of the gold. Collins thinks that when I confronted Gus and he couldn't tell me where the gold was, I snatched his cane and struck him on the head, killing him."

Bud looked from Snow to Joanna. "What gold?"

"The miners paid the two Chinese doctors who ran this apothecary for their services in gold from their mines, and the docs have buried it somewhere around here," Snow said.

Joanna sat up a little straighter. "How do you know about all that?"

"Alex told me. Finding the real killer is a simple matter, really."

Joanna unfolded her legs. "How so?"

"Find the person who's been trying to scare you off with those notes, and we've found the killer."

"What notes?" Bud asked.

"Someone's been telling me to leave in a series of notes. They cut the brake line on my Ural and actually came in the apartment and wrote on the hall wall," Joanna said.

"That's it then," Snow said. "Who has a key to your apartment?"

"I was given two keys when I arrived, and I gave one to Alex."

"Who gave you the keys?" Snow questioned.

"The mayor."

Snow rocked back in his chair. "Bingo. Now, all we have to do is show that he had means, motive, and opportunity, or prove that he's the one who's been writing those notes. Do you have any sense that the mayor was actually behind the notes?"

Joanna thought about this. "He showed up unexpectedly right after Alex fell from the loft."

"Wait," Bud started, but she waved him to silence.

"Right after his fall, he was still on the floor, and he whispered the word cell phone. And just before the railing gave, he said there were footprints in the dust up there."

Bud held up one finger.

"Yes, Bud, what is it?"

"When I was checking out the area as you asked, I found a cell phone. The face is cracked, and I think the battery is dead," Bud said, and pulled the phone in question from his pocket.

Joanna took the phone from the teen and plugged it in to charge.

"Bud, is the ladder leading up to the loft safe?" Snow asked.

"I think so."

Snow got to his feet. "Let's go check out those footprints."

Rusty followed the three downstairs and into the apothecary, where they stared up at the loft.

"I'll go." Snow said, pulling out his own cell phone. "I'll take some pictures."

When he stepped off the ladder to the loft, he stopped.

"I see two sets, big and small," Snow said, and took several pictures, then climbed down. "I'll assume that the larger prints belong to Alex, so we're looking for someone with small feet."

Bud laughed. "All we have to do is break into the mayor's house and steal a pair of his shoes."

"I'm more for a direct approach," Snow responded.

Joanna ran a hand through her hair. "What would that be?"

Snow shrugged. "Tell him what we think and watch him squirm."

Joanna let out a breath. "Okay, let's go." She took Rusty back up to the apartment and, with Snow and Bud, climbed into the cab of her truck.

"Shouldn't we be making a plan?" Bud asked.

"The idea is to get him to incriminate himself or catch him in a lie," Snow said.

"It's getting late," Joanna interrupted. "Let's go to his house first. Bud, do you know where he lives?"

"As a matter of fact, I do. He hired me to help organize his garage."

"I think it would be best if you two let me do the talking," Joanna said. "If anything goes sideways, Snow, that will be your cue to step in."

"What do you want me to do?" Bud asked.

"You'll be witness to whatever transpires. Just let us do the talking."

A short drive later, Joanna pulled up to the curb in front of a modest Craftsman home with a carport.

Chapter Thirty-seven

The mayor opened the door just far enough to look out, looking surprised and looking a little frazzled.

"Ms. Bright," he said, and looked past her at Snow and Bud. "What can I do for you? Is everything all right?"

"No, it's not. Can we come in and talk?"

He brought the door to a near close, looking behind it, then opened the door wider. "Sure, come in. Can I get you something to drink?"

Joanna walked into the living room. "This isn't a social visit."

"I see," the mayor said. "Does it have something to do with the apothecary?"

Snow and Bud remained standing while Joanna sat in a wingback chair facing the mayor, who sat on the couch,

"I'll get right to the point," Joanna said. "Are you aware that Sheriff Collins, just before he resigned, submitted a file to the state district attorney's office claiming that I killed Gus Hasselbacker?"

"I was aware that he'd filed a report with the state DA but had no idea what it was about."

"It asserted that I killed Gus over his knowledge of the whereabouts of some hidden miners' gold. You are aware of the story, aren't you?"

"Of course. Its part of the lore that I'm hoping will make the apothecary a tourist attraction."

"I didn't kill Gus, but I've been getting threatening notes telling me to leave Dungeness Bay. I believe that whoever has been sending me those notes may also be Gus's murderer and possibly responsible for the disappearance of Thayer Spelling."

"You're telling me all this why?"

Snow stepped around to face the mayor. "We're here because we think that you've been sending those notes."

"What in the world? Why would I do such a thing?"

"Millions in gold would be your motive, and Gus's cane would be the means, which you struck him down with. The storm would be the opportunity, completely destroying any evidence that you confronted and killed him, and, as you know, his body was taken to the Lincoln City morgue, where it was examined by the assistant medical examiner."

"This is absurd, and I resent the accusation that I killed anyone, and for what? Gold?" The mayor bristled. "No. I want you out of my house, now."

Snow didn't move. "I have the day, date, and approximate time of Gus's murder. Where were you six days ago?"

"He was with me."

All heads turned and the mayor came to his feet when Stan emerged out of the hall.

The blood drained from the mayor's face, and he began to sag. Stan rushed to his side and walked him to the couch.

Snow exchanged looks with Joanna. "Mayor Ritter, you're gay?"

Ritter looked up. "Yes, and I'm pleading with you to keep this a secret. In a conservative town like this—" He shook his head. "I'd have to leave the area, the state."

Joanna touched Snow on the shoulder and sat on a coffee table facing the mayor. "Calvin—Mayor Ritter—I believe we have proof that you were the one who cut through the railing on the loft that Alex fell through. It seems an incredible coincidence that you showed up for no reason minutes after his fall."

The mayor looked over at Stan before turning back to Joanna. "I was dropping by to see how you were getting along. What proof?"

"Footprints in the dust."

Snow stepped forward, producing the photo of the footprint he'd taken.

"I think this is your shoe print."

"This is ridiculous. Your proof that I've been sending these threatening notes is a shoe print in some dust. Well, let's just look at my shoes right now."

Reaching down, he removed his shoes from both feet. "There," he said, holding them out for Snow to examine. "I tell you what. Take them out to the apothecary and put them next to the print made in the dust. I have small feet, but not as small as what appears in that photo."

"Calvin has an alibi," Stan interjected, "and I can tell you right now that his shoes won't match the prints in the dust. So what now?"

Joanna looked over at Snow, who shrugged. "Back to the drawing board, I guess. "

The three piled back in the truck and they made the drive back to the apothecary, silent with their own thoughts.

"Hey guys," Bud said. "I have a scenario, a different approach to all this."

"I don't know. Every time I try to visualize the killer I come up with a blank," Joanna said.

"Honestly, I'm all ears Bud," Snow said. "What are you thinking?"

"First, I think that the person who killed Gus is the same person who killed Thayer, and I think you're right," Bud said, looking at Snow. "If we can find the person who's been sending Joanna those notes, we'll have our killer. Problem is, we need a medical examiner to look at Thayer's body."

They arrived at the apothecary and Joanna parked at the foot of the steps. She went upstairs to let Rusty out, then was joined by Bud and Snow, who greeted her grinning from ear to ear.

She eyed them both. "Okay guys, what's up?"

Bud gave Snow a nod. "Mack, as you know, works part-time at the medical supply house in Lincoln City. What you don't know is he is also an assistant medical examiner. I can get him down here in his official capacity to look at Thayer's body. He can identify her by dental records. More importantly, he can determine cause of death as well as approximately how long she's been dead. Tell her what you're thinking, Bud."

As Snow spoke, he sat down in one corner of the couch, Joanna in the other. Bud stood in front of them and began to pace.

"We'll call the murderer Suspect X. Whoever they are knows about the gold, and that's motive. That same someone, Suspect X, becomes aware through conversations with Gus Hasselbacker that Thayer Spelling is putting together clues she's gotten from interviews and has come up with three possible locations of the gold. When Suspect X presses Gus to reveal the three locations, he won't spill the beans. Gus is furious that Suspect X would try to squeeze the locations out of him and threatens to tell Thayer and the Sheriff.

"Suspect X is now pushed into a corner and decides that Gus needs to be silenced. To this end, Gus is lured down the trail that goes from the apothecary to the smokehouse. Suspect X tells him that he or she has figured out the location of the gold and that they can get it together, leaving Thayer out of it. All Thayer would know is that her three potential locations were a bust. Fast forward to the storm. China Bluff is being buffeted by wind and rain. Gus shows up and Suspect X snatches his cane and bashes him on the head, figuring that the storm will cover evidence of foul play. Now all Suspect X needs to do is watch Thayer, and when she goes to the location, Suspect X strikes again. And there it is," Bud concluded.

Joanna moaned. "How would Suspect X know when Thayer was heading to the correct location?"

Bud nodded. "Good question. The assumption is that she would go to the most likely location first."

Snow turned to face Joanna. "Mack will be able to determine a time frame around the two killings."

"Your friend Mack will be able to confirm my theory that Thayer was also killed with Gus's cane. Suspect X probably figured that if the body was found, it would appear that Gus killed her," Bud said.

Snow picked up the narrative. "The official medical examiner's report would indicate Gus as Thayer's killer and exonerate you. We can assume that the notes telling you to leave here are written by someone who can't check out the three possible locations for the gold because you're somehow in the way."

Bud stopped pacing. "Wait. What if they think you know where the gold is?"

Chapter Thirty-Eight

Joanna shook her head. "Why would they tell me to get out of here if they thought I knew where the gold was? That doesn't make sense."

"My theory makes perfect sense," Bud said. "If you kept a briefcase with a million dollars in your house and your house caught on fire, of course, the first thing you'd grab would be that briefcase."

"You're thinking that if I respond to the threats and leave then I'd grab the gold and go."

Snow rocked back and forth a few times. "What you're saying, Bud makes total sense and explains why the threats have gone from notes to cutting the brake line on the Ural and sawing partway through the loft rail. The level of the threat is escalating." He then addressed Joanna. "When they broke into your house and wrote a threat on your hall wall, they were showing that you weren't safe here."

Joanna got up, needing to take a short break. "I'm going to get us some beers."

When she returned with three bottles, she broke up a heated conversation between Bud and Snow. "Hey, guys. The problem is that we still don't know who Suspect X is. All we know is that this person is behind the threatening notes."

Bud began to nod his head.

Joanna said, "All right Bud, you've got the floor. What are you thinking?"

"You two might not be aware that when a movie scene takes place in a field or, say, a jungle, special people, usually locals, are hired to beat the bushes and drive out the snakes."

Snow hadn't touched his beer and set the full bottle on the floor, a motion that didn't go unnoticed by Joanna.

"I'm so sorry for my lapse in memory. Can I get you a cup of coffee or anything?"

"No thanks," Snow said graciously.

"Bud, what you're proposing is that we set a trap?" Joanna asked.

Bud snapped his fingers. "Exactly."

"Oh, boy," Snow said. "I'll take that cup of coffee now."

"Cream and sugar? And what kind of trap, Bud?" Joanna asked.

"Both," Snow said before turning to Bud. "You're batting a thousand so far, kid. What kind of trap are you thinking of?"

Bud drained his bottle and handed it to Joanna as she headed for the kitchen.

"Find the gold in the most public and obvious way possible."

Joanna returned with a mug of coffee, which she handed to Snow, then turned to Bud. "Shoot, I should have thought of that; simply find the gold."

"No, no. Just pretend that you do," Bud said. "You two might not realize it, but in World War Two, there was a ghost army that consisted of balloon tanks that fooled the Germans into thinking that the allies were massing for a major assault."

"What the hell are you saying? Can you possibly explain without getting into history?" Joanna rubbed her temple.

"Joanna, do you know for sure the date that the DA's investigator will arrive in Dungeness Bay?" Snow asked.

"Based on what Sheriff Collins told me, and I believe him, he'll be here in four days."

"Great. That's when you're going to have a grand opening for the apothecary. For the next four days, you're going to let it slip that a special announcement will be made about a discovery," Bud said.

Snow laughed. "Genius, pure genius. Joanna, for the next four days you're going to act as though you found the gold. Bud can be knocking around the apothecary for anyone who might be spying, and I'm sure that if we let the mayor in on this he'll play along. But how do we spring the trap?" Snow wondered out loud

Joanna drained her second bottle of beer. "I've got it. Bud, you said that you do metalwork and small woodcrafts. You're going to build a metal strongbox. Make it look old. Then you're going to create a fancy wood structure to hold the ancient chest for the grand reveal."

"Literally, the grand opening will be on the day the investigator arrives. The day before, you need to make a big production of the surprise that the contents are in the chest, which is in the apothecary. From the moment you make that announcement—and the mayor can drop by to make it seem more real—we can expect a break-in," Bud said.

Snow's facial expression was going back and forth between serious contemplation and a silly grin.

"Okay Joanna, between now and the big day, you finish the deck, teach your tai chi classes, and just basically go about your business. For effect, and to ensure that whoever is watching gets the feeling that something big is about to happen, we can get the mayor to make a late-night visit.

"Tomorrow, I'm going to make a big show of leaving town, then return to my campsite in the woods. Before I leave, I'll pick up three walkie-talkies, one for each of us. After the mayor's evening visit, the threats will likely increase in number and intensity. And for sure, keep Rusty close. He's a hundred pounds of intimidation. I'm in the woods tonight, then off tomorrow."

Snow stepped forward and gave Joanna a hug, assured her one last time that everything would be fine, and headed out.

Joanna turned to face Bud. "Until you came up with your theory, I was drawing a blank, sure I was going to hang for a murder I didn't commit. Thank you."

Bud looked at his feet, then up at Joanna. "I have a favor to ask."

"Shoot."

"Could I sleep here in the living room?" Bud asked, holding up a hand. "Just until I find a place."

"Alex is still in California, so you can sleep in his room. Besides, I'd feel better with you up here until this over."

Chapter Thirty-nine

Joanna finished her early morning tai chi and qigong and took Rusty for a run down the beach, pleased that Bud was already busy in the apothecary. She felt good about the plan they had made the night before to draw out the killer. Everything proposed made sense. Still, some details were missing. How would the suspect get to the chest and the strongbox? Would she have to leave the doors to the apothecary open? And if she did, wouldn't that make the suspect see it as a trap? But if the doors were closed and locked, the only way into the apothecary would be through the dumbwaiter. That would mean they would have to break into the apartment.

She paused and watched Rusty play tag with the tide but was distracted by more questions. She sat down on a giant log that had washed up on the beach. How was it going to work out when the DA's investigator arrived? Would they tell him their plan, and if they did, would he be willing to stick around and wait to see what happened? Then she was back to the question of how far to let the suspect go. Wouldn't they have to have a representative of the law on the premises to make the arrest, which would be Chuck Cowdrey?

Would he be willing to go along with the plan? When the same questions came around again, Joanna knew she was dealing with drunken monkeys and she would need to clear her mind. She needed to be proactive and make a list that she could fall back on. After all, she only had three days to get all the people in play.

She slid off the log, and Rusty ran to her side. "Come on, big guy. Let's head back to the apartment."

When she turned to look up at China Bluff and the back of the apothecary, she saw Bud waving at her. "Come on Rusty, race you to the top!"

The minute she reached the trail, Rusty knew their destination and easily shot past her. He waited for her at the top, Bud at his side.

Pumping her arms, Joanna ran the switchbacks that led to the top of the bluff. Out of breath, she walked over, bent in half, and pulled Rusty into a hug.

"What's going on, Bud?"

"I found something in the apothecary you need to see."

"What is it?"

"I'm not sure, but I have a hunch."

"Okay, let's take a look."

Rusty followed until he saw where they were going and ran past them into the apothecary.

They walked through the herb shop, back past the storage rooms, until they stood facing the living quarters.

"Okay, what am I looking for?"

"Tell me what you see."

"Is this really necessary?"

"Yeah, I think so."

"Fine. It's the living area," Joanna said, becoming a little animated. "There on the left is a sleeping platform. On the right is an old wood stove, the kind you can cook on. I'd say the entire space is around eight feet wide and sixteen feet deep. At the end is a wooden chair and to the immediate right of the chair is a series of shelves." She looked over at Bud. "How am I doing?"

"You're getting warm."

"There is a counter I suspect they ate off of, and below that counter are two shelves."

"Stop. Let's take a close look at that bottom shelf," Bud said.

"Come on Bud. What the hell is so important?"

They walked past the stove to the continuous counter.

"Looks like the shelves stop here." With a knuckle, Bud thumped on the wall at the end of the shelves. "When I pushed on this bottom shelf, I noticed it was loose and I could pull it up, like so. Notice that the shelf is hinged to the wall and conceals a compartment."

Joanna looked at Bud, impressed. "Gee Bud, it looks to me like you've found a hidden compartment."

"Look closer."

Joanna did. She reached in and pulled out an eight-by-sixteen sheet of thick paper covered with lines of Chinese characters.

"What do you make of that?" Bud asked.

"It could be a menu, for all I know."

Bud made a face. "No, it's a page out of a bookkeeper's log."

"You read Chinese?"

"No, but I've done my share of bookkeeping. The lines and the headings are a dead giveaway."

Joanna flipped the paper over.

"You're not quite getting it," Bud said. "Yesterday you mentioned the story about gold. I think the Chinese doctors were tracking how much came in, and if I'm not mistaken, at least one of those characters at the top is a date. You need to get this translated, and I know who can do that for you."

"You're right. This could tell us how much gold was taken in, but I've got my own translator. Oh, and Bud, if you find anything else of interest, no more guessing games. Just tell me."

Bud dug into his back pocket and pulled out a single sheet of paper. "Here's the list of materials you asked for. It includes what I'll need to build the chest, and I'll let you know about the strongbox. I'm going to look for some metal around here that's already aged."

Before Joanna walked away, Bud spoke again. "You don't like the stories and guessing games. I get it. I'm sorry."

Joanna nodded and left Bud poking around. With Rusty at her heels, she headed for the root cellar and took the tunnel to the apothecary's basement.

"Doc Hay, are you down here?"

"Of course. I see you found Long On's ledger."

"Only one sheet," Joanna said and held it out. "Can you translate it?"

"Did you intend on asking such a silly question?"

"Sorry, sorry. What does it say?"

"Lay it on the table."

The shimmering image of Doc Hay followed her to the table in the middle of the room and then appeared to bend over the page.

"This is indeed from Long On's gold ledger."

"Gold ledger?"

"We learned the art of assaying and created a kiln and a mold."

"You melted down the gold?"

"Yes, into bricks. Gold from the miners came in different forms. We spent many hours, learning by mishap, mostly."

"How many bricks, would you say?"

"Over half a century, I never kept track, mind you. That was Long On's job. You could say he was the mathematician, and I was the herb healer."

"How many bricks, Doc?"

"Thousands."

Joanna staggered back two steps. "What?"

"Perhaps thousands and thousands."

She took several more steps until she was leaning against the wall, and then slid to the floor.

"How much did these bricks weigh?"

"No idea. But you might find a bit of mold in that pile of straw."

Flabbergasted, Joanna pushed herself up and walked to the far corner of the basement. She felt around in the pile of straw, finally pulling out a crude mold. With her cell phone, she took pictures from several angles. "Looks about three by five inches and four inches deep. My god, thousands of these would be worth millions. Thanks, Doc."

Still, in shock over this new revelation, Joanna walked to her living room and sat in her club chair with her journal, but didn't open it. She mentally poured over the questions that had confounded her on the beach but decided the journal was the best place for those thoughts.

Dear Journal,

I have so many questions that must be answered in the next two days, and now I've found the reason someone has killed for the miners' gold. But most amazing thing is that I believe I've established a relationship with an actual ghost. The fact is that this gold ledger tells me that there is a good chance that whoever murdered Gus and Thayer is the same person that has been sending me notes to get out. Snow says that once the mayor stops by, pretending to approve my revealing of something I've found, I can expect the threats to increase in intensity and frequency.

From all this planning, I found two weak links. Chuck Cowdrey, the deputy, now sheriff, with the resignation of Jesse Collins, and the district attorney's agent. Also, I feel the need to recruit some of the locals that I have met to help catch the killer.

Chapter Forty

Joanna set pen down, leaned back in her chair, and gazed across the room. After shaking herself out of her thoughts, she ended her entry: *I'll invite those I trust up for tea and explain the plan.*

Joanna walked back to her room. Instead of putting her journal under the mattress, she placed it on the nightstand and then exited the apartment. She was headed for the apothecary when Snow rode up on his motorcycle.

"Your timing is excellent. I'm inviting some of the locals I've met to assist in our plan."

"Are you sure you want to do that?" Snow asked.

"I've learned that there are thousands of bricks of gold, no doubt worth millions, somewhere around here."

Snow hung his helmet from a side mirror." Are you sure? How did you find out?"

"Bud discovered a page from a ledger that the doctors were using to track their gold with, and I had it translated." Joanna smiled to herself; it was only a partial lie. "I think that whoever falls for our trap may be more determined than we first imagined because they might have the entire ledger. I only have one page."

"I brought the walkie-talkies as promised and will be riding out of town and returning to my camp. I won't be back until after dark. You and Bud will be on your own."

"I'll make a list of potential volunteers and leave it in your tent."

"I'll contact you with the walkie when I get back to camp," Snow said.

Joanna watched him ride off, then walked into the apothecary and invited Bud up for an early lunch. After eating, Bud jumped up, taking his plate, cup, and silverware to the sink.

"The rice and vegetables were great. Can I help with the dishes?"

"I'll do the dishes later. Right now, I want you to deliver some invitations. Let's go into the living room. I've made up a list of people who I'm hoping will want to help with our plan to catch the killer."

"What are you thinking, and who can you trust?" Bud asked.

"That ledger page translated out to millions of dollars of gold. I don't want to take any chances of the murderer getting away. Plus, the DA's investigator will be here, and I want to impress him with our plan. I figure we could have five people, like someone to block the driveway. Snow is in the forest. Then there's the back door. Because we'll lock the front doors of the apothecary, the only way in will be with the dumbwaiter, so I'll need someone up in the apartment. Bud, you and I will be in the apothecary, probably along with the investigator."

"When are we going to have this get-together?"

"I've got three days, so tomorrow evening," Joanna responded, pulling the list out of her pocket and handing it to Bud. "What do you think?"

"The mayor and Stan, Terry Chambers from the bar and grill, Eric from the hardware store, and Lisa Posey and Bobby Alvarez. I think they're all trustworthy. You going to lay out the plan?"

"That's what I'm doing. Take my truck. The meeting will be at ten o'clock. Don't tell them anything about the plan but make sure they know it's important."

Joanna went back up to the apartment and jotted down how she thought the plan should be laid out and what she would tell her volunteers.

When Rusty climbed out from under the desk, she knew she had company. She walked out onto the landing in time to watch two motorcycles roll into the parking area.

She slapped her side. "Rusty, come." He led the way and waited for her at the bottom of the steps. She relaxed when they pulled off their helmets, recognizing Mack and John.

She gave each a hug and then looked at John. "Where's Alex?"

"He's staying at the San Francisco VA for a couple of days. He was having some vision problems—something left over from the fall."

Joanna felt a pang of guilt but shook it off.

"We got a call from Snow that you had some kind of plan to catch Gus's killer and thought you might need a little strong arm," Mack said, and then lowered his voice. "You have a body you want me to look at? I've got a copy of the ME's report on Gus that you might want to look at first, then we can go out and look at the body."

Joanna filled Mack in as they walked up the steps to her apartment. "What should I be looking for in this report? My understanding is that Gus was killed by a blow to the head."

"Second page, cause of death."

Joanna flipped to the second page and scanned down halfway. "Blunt trauma."

"Go down two lines," Mack said.

"If my interpretation is correct," Joanna said, "the killing blow was located at the top center of the skull."

"Correct. Now go back to the first page and tell me how tall Gus was."

She flipped back. "Six foot, three inches. Okay, what am I not seeing?"

"There was no angle to the strike. It was made with his cane all right, but the person who hit him had to be taller than six foot three."

"You're sure about this?"

"I was there when Austin did the autopsy," Mack said. "The question is, who do you know that's over six foot three?"

Joanna looked over at Bud. "Stan Hunter, the vet, but he had an alibi." Joanna ran a hand through her hair. "I just can't believe he'd kill for gold. This changes everything."

Bud touched her on the arm. "It doesn't change a thing. Whoever wrote those notes for you to get out and killed Gus and Thayer will come for the gold and fall into our trap.

Chapter Forty-one

John rubbed his chin. "This Stan guy, how tall is he?"

"At least six foot six," Joanna said.

"What was his alibi?" John continued.

"He said he was with his partner."

"Wife or lady friend? I say we have a talk with her."

"Stan's gay," Bud blurted out.

John raised an eyebrow. "That doesn't mean shit."

"Wow," Bud retorted. "What makes you an expert?"

"Because I'm gay," John said and took a step toward Bud.

Joanna remembered Snow saying that John was a brawler and stepped between the two before things escalated.

John held up both hands but didn't step back. "Tell you what kid. I'd beat the crap out of you just like a straight guy."

Joanna reached out and put a hand on John's chest. "That's enough."

"My point is that Stan being gay doesn't make him more or less inclined to commit murder," John said.

"Point taken," Joanna said.

Bud took a few steps back. "Maybe not, but it makes him more vulnerable."

Joanna could feel John pushing against her arm. "Kid, you've got about sixty seconds to make sense of that."

"Okay, okay. What if Gus were blackmailing Stan over something?"

John took a step back. "Like what?"

Bud looked over at Joanna. "Stan and the mayor are an item. When we confronted the mayor with the idea that he was the killer, he nearly fainted. Said that if it got out that he was gay he would be ruined. What if Gus had a beef with the mayor, knew he was gay, and threatened to out him? If, as you say, gays are just people, what would you do to preserve your way of life, protect your lover?"

John nodded. "You're not as dumb as you look. So, what do we know about Gus?"

"I know that Alex came to Dungeness Bay to help him out. The guy was broke," Mack said.

"I met Gus at the San Francisco VA," John said. "I was in for their treatment program and Gus was getting his leg fixed. That was about two years ago."

"That was about the time the mayor was elected," Bud said.

"He ran on keeping a small town small, you know, not letting in big business. There was some stink about something just after Ritter became mayor."

"I think I know what that something was," Mack said. "Alex told me that Gus had approached him about investing in a development project to build beachfront condominiums in Dungeness Bay. Gus sank his last penny into the project. I don't know for certain, but Calvin Ritter wears two hats: one as mayor, and one as a city planner. I'd be willing to wager that he put the kibosh on the condominium project and that of course would leave Gus high, dry, and broke."

Joanna handed back the ME's report on Gus. "What about the small footprints? Stan certainly doesn't have small feet. And what about all the notes telling me to get out? I'm more confused now than ever before. If it were a case of blackmail that led Stan to murder Gus and to protect the mayor, why the notes, and why would he cut through the rail around the loft?"

Mack glanced at his watch. "I've got to get back to Lincoln City. Let's have a look at the body."

"It's in the bottom of the old smokehouse. We figure it's been covered in ashes for a couple of months," Joanna said.

They all headed over to the smokehouse, John and Mack removed the plank floor.

Joanna handed Mack a flashlight.

Mack took one look, straightened up, and turned to Joanna. "Here's the problem. I can't move the body because I'd be disturbing evidence. I can't even touch the body," he said, and got down on his hands and knees. "Head's twisted, and the way the shoulders are canted, I'd say she wasn't pushed or dragged, but fell. I see evidence of blunt force trauma to the head, and from the indentation, I'd say she was hit with something round."

Mack stood up and brushed off his knees. "I couldn't begin to guess at how long she's been dead without moving the body. Guess I haven't been much help," he said apologetically.

"Don't worry about it," Joanna said. "I'm still setting a trap for the killer. Will you and John come back for tomorrow's meeting?"

Mack looked at John, who gave him a nod. "You can plan on it."

She watched them ride off. Bud went back into the apothecary and continued his work on the metal chest.

Chapter Forty-two

The sound of a knock at the apartment door rousted Rusty who ran to the door and then back to Joanna, waiting for a command.

"All right, Rusty. We've got someone arriving early. Time to be on your best behavior."

She opened the door to greet Mayor Ritter.

"I know I'm early," he said, "but I wanted a moment alone with you."

"Please, come in and have a seat. Can I get you anything to drink?"

"No, thank you. I'm hoping whatever you have in mind for this meeting will not expose Stan or myself as gay."

"Mayor Ritter, I can assure you of two things. First, I have no intention of outing either of you, and second, your being gay is in no way an issue for me," Joanna said and smiled. "I believe in live and let live."

"Thank you, I appreciate that. Enough said. Now, what's this meeting all about? Bud said it was important and that there would be a number of business owners in attendance."

"I can only say that this meeting is very important for me, and I'd like to wait until everyone has arrived to explain."

"Fair enough."

Joanna was saved from making small talk by a knock at the door. She was relieved and a bit taken by surprise when Terry Chambers stepped up and gave her a hug.

"I was a little disappointed that you didn't ask me to bring my chili." He winked, walked across the floor, and shook the mayor's hand. "Any idea what this meeting is all about?"

The mayor shook his head. "Your guess is as good as mine."

Lisa and Bobby came together. They found the door ajar and

knocked before letting themselves in. Finally, Eric arrived, followed by Mack and John.

Joanna was pleased that Rusty had parked himself under the desk. She clapped her hands and asked everyone to take a seat.

"I know it's late, and I want to thank every one of you for responding on such short notice."

Bud came in, closed the door as quietly as possible, and leaned against it. Terry pointed at him. "There's the messenger now." A few chuckles emerged.

"I apologize for the way you were contacted and hope you'll understand when I explain."

Joanna noticed Mack approaching from the corner of her eye with a glass of water and took a grateful sip. She took the moment to exhale a calming breath.

"This is Mack, a friend of Alex Jenner, who is currently in the San Francisco VA recuperating from a fall he took while in the apothecary."

Joanna took another sip of water. "What you may not know is that when Sheriff Jesse Collins resigned, he submitted a file to the state district attorney listing me as a person of interest in the murder of Gus Hasselbacker."

Joanna looked at everyone in the room. "Let me state now without equivocation that I did not kill Gus Hasselbacker. But the person who did, the murderer, has been threatening me with notes demanding that I leave. The reason I ask you here is that I have a plan that will capture the murderer."

Joanna looked at Bud, who moved away from the door.

"Before I tell you this plan, I want you to know that anyone who feels uncomfortable with this may leave."

No one moved.

"Thank you. This plan is based on what I understand has been folklore about miners' gold buried somewhere in or around the apothecary. In the few days I've been in Dungeness Bay, I've stumbled on proof beyond the shadow of a doubt that there are millions of dollars of gold buried somewhere nearby. I believe that whoever has been sending me these notes is privy to that same information, but, like myself, does not know where it is located."

Eric raised a hand to interrupt the narrative and then stood. "You've certainly piqued my interest, but what's the connection to the Gus's murder?"

Joanna tried to catch the mood of her guests and figured that Eric had summed it up, that she'd managed to pique the group's interest.

"The caretaker of the apothecary before me was writer Thayer Spelling, who was doing interviews for a documentary about the early days of Dungeness Bay.

"In her research, she gathered clues that led her to believe that the gold was located in one of three locations. Gus was working closely with Thayer, and whoever killed Gus did so after he refused to divulge his knowledge of the locations."

Terry asked, "You're saying that someone killed Gus for a million dollars?"

"No, not a million. I found a page from the original owners' gold ledger that put the amount at roughly twenty-five million."

Terry gave a short, low whistle.

"Remember that neither I nor the murderer knows the location of the gold but we both know the amount, and that was enough for this person to murder Gus and, I believe, kill Thayer Spelling."

Lisa Posey stood. "So, what we have is a highly motivated murderer?"

"That's correct. More than just leaving notes, this person cut the brake line on my Ural motorcycle and broke into my apartment here and left a note on my hall wall."

Lisa, still standing, asked, "You've called us here because you have a plan to catch the killer and you want us to help?"

Joanna nodded. "Again, if anyone wants to leave, please feel free to do so."

Again, no one moved.

Joanna stated, "Our plan is simple, really. I'm going to convince the murderer that I've found the gold. Bud is building a wooden chest that will hold a very old-looking strongbox that supposedly contains a sample of several gold bricks that I am going to present to the mayor, along with a map showing the location of the rest of the gold."

Eric shot to his feet. "What do you want from us?"

"It's my belief that the murderer has killed twice and will not hesitate to use whatever means necessary to get the map to the location of the gold and get away. Rather than confront such a desperate person, my plan is to let them take the map and seal off any escape. To this end, Sheriff Chuck Cowdrey and the investigator sent by the state DA will be present."

The evening ended with a lot of small talk and expressed support for Joanna. She felt good but stopped the mayor, the last to leave.

She touched him on the shoulder as he approached the door. "Mayor Ritter."

"I'd be pleased if you would call me Calvin."

She bobbed her head. "Calvin, I need to have Sheriff Cowdrey present when we corner the murderer, but I had a bad run-in with him a couple of days ago when I used his phone."

"Don't say another word," Ritter said. "I'll smooth things over for you and make sure he's jolly on the spot."

Chapter Forty-three

"If I understand my role correctly," the mayor said. "I'm to visit you at the apothecary tomorrow around two o'clock?"

"Yes, and because we don't know who the murderer is, we need to get the word out that something big is about to happen. Make sure that you let the city council know, plus your secretary and anyone in your circle."

"You can count on me," he said and walked out the door.

Mack walked up behind Joanna and as soon as the mayor was gone. "You didn't exactly give us assignments."

"I didn't forget you guys," Joanna said. "The apothecary will be locked up tight, leaving the only way to get in through the lift. The murderer will know this and break into the apartment. I'd like you and John to spend the night. You in my bed, John in the spare bedroom."

"You want us to grab the killer?"

"No, no confrontation. Your role is to let us know when they enter the apartment, and, if necessary, block their exit."

"Now I get it. I couldn't figure out why the request for throat mics and earbuds."

"There'll be no talking, so how will they work?" Joanna asked.

"If I touch my throat mic, it will send a static buzz into your ear. When the killer enters the apartment, I'll send you some static."

"Mack, I appreciate what you and John are doing so much. Can you guys hang around until then?"

"Yeah. I was talking to John, and we were thinking we could help with the deck. You know, make it look like life as normal."

"You're on. Bud has fixed his Karmann Ghia and is taking me into town. You can use the truck to get any materials. I've got a running tab with Eric Ward, owner of the hardware store; he's got lumber and everything. The two of you can stay in the spare bedroom tonight. Bud's been staying there, but he can sleep on the couch."

Mack gave a short laugh. "I understand that Snow is bivouacked out in the woods."

"He's watching the parking area."

The next morning, Joanna pulled on her Joseph robe, assembled a stack of clothes, then padded down the short hall to the bathroom. She noticed that the door to the spare bedroom was open, the room empty. She was pleased that the two men were already up and probably working on the deck.

She climbed in the shower, let the hot water pound on her shoulders, and went over the plan. Her second tai chi class would be the day before the investigator arrived, and the deck wouldn't be finished by then, so the class would be held on the grass next to the gravel parking area.

Bud needed to complete the wooden chest so that it could be on display in the front of the apothecary. The entire class would see it and word would get out.

When the shower water cooled off, Joanna was reminded that she needed to get a bigger hot water heater.

She stepped out of the bathroom and was hit with the aroma of coffee that wafted down the hall, followed by the smell of bacon and something else she couldn't put a finger on.

"I thought you'd never get out of the shower." Terry laughed. "Are those prunes or fingers?"

"Terry," Joanna said, surprised. "I'm glad to see you, but what are you doing here?"

"You've already got your hands full, and what, now you have to cook for John, Mack, and Bud, on top of it all?"

"What about the bar?"

"Don't worry about that. It's taken care of. My people have been working for me for years, and Kat is super dependable."

Bud burst through the door. "Joanna, you about ready to go?"

He said and looked over at Terry. "Great breakfast by the way." He turned back to Joanna. "I'm headed into town for supplies and can take you around but need to get back as soon as possible if I'm going to finish the chest."

"Bud, you go work on the chest," Terry said. "Joanna, you sit down and eat. I'll take you into town."

Joanna sat down to a plate of bacon, eggs, and hot coffee. Homemade muffins were the aroma she hadn't been able to figure out. When Terry called Rusty to his bowl of kibble, she took the opportunity to admire the broad shoulders of the man who seemed to have her best interest at heart. When he returned to the counter for his cup of coffee, she made sure he didn't catch her staring.

Terry came over and sat across from her, sipping his coffee. "Where are we headed?"

"You know that you don't have to do this—breakfast and taking me around."

"I know I can be a little headstrong. Just give me the word and I'll back off."

She put her fork down, reached across the table, and took Terry's hand. "Your spirit is so refreshing, and just what I need," she said, looking into his blue eyes. "No, I need you at my side through this."

He placed a hand on top of hers. "You'll get through this Joanna, and the community of Dungeness Bay will be better for you being here."

Joanna had been overwhelmed and emotional since she had arrived in Dungeness Bay, and she couldn't hold back her tears. As they blurred her vision, she lurched from her chair turned her back, burying her face in her hands. Terry got up and slowly walked around, pulling her into a gentle hug.

Chapter Forty-four

Joanna made her way to the bathroom to regain her composure. Embarrassed, and not knowing what to say, she was relieved that Terry wasn't waiting in the kitchen. Followed closely by Rusty, she descended the steps, stopping in the middle. Terry was leaning on the front of an Austin-Healey, just like the one she and K. C. had.

When she crossed the gravel lot, he opened the door. "Your taxi awaits."

She looked at Rusty, who was waiting for a command.

"It's all right," Terry said. "The dog rides for free." Then he pulled the passenger seat forward. "Come on, boy."

Rusty didn't move.

"Get in; you're invited," Joanna said.

Rusty bounded in and lay down.

She climbed in and asked, "Nineteen sixty-three?"

Terry started the engine. "Good eye. How did you know?"

"When I lived in Carmel, I had a Healey just like this, except it was blue. Where in the world—"

He cut her off. "I know, where did the owner of a bar and grill in a tiny town like Dungeness Bay get the wherewithal for a Classic Austin-Healey? Remember our conversation from the other day, when you dropped in for food?"

"Yes, you mentioned qualifying for the world games in judo but not making the Olympics."

"I had sponsors through about six years of training and qualifying. When I didn't make the grade for the big show, things kind of dried up, but not before I pocketed a bundle and acquired the Healey."

Joanna hesitated, then changed topics. "Terry, I'm so embarrassed about my little breakdown."

"Don't give it a second thought. I cried like a baby when I didn't qualify for the Olympics. Then I got my shit together, went back to school, got an MBA, moved on to Portland's Culinary College, finally took up residence in Dungeness Bay, and bought the bar, where I make a chili to die for. Now, where to?"

"The Chocolate Factory. Lisa Posey said I could use her shop to make Chinese five-spice chocolate truffles. From there, we're heading to—and you're invited, of course—a gossip fest at the Outpouring, where we'll probably catch lunch."

"I have a better idea," Terry said. "I drop you off at the Chocolate Factory. Then, you head to the Outpouring and spread some rumors. I'm no good at gossip, so while you're doing that, I'll get some groceries, then take the two of you back to your apartment, where I'll demonstrate my culinary skills and treat you to Coquilles St. Jacques à la Chambers.

"Sounds great," Joanna responded enthusiastically. "We can have the five-spice truffles for dessert."

After Joanna made a batch of the truffles, Lisa and Joanna crossed the street to the Outpouring, surprised when they asked to speak with the owner and were told that Cheryl was home sick. They chatted back and forth over coffee about the special event that would be taking place at the apothecary, making sure that they could easily be overheard. Finally, when they were running out of gossip about the event, Terry came in.

"I love your car, but I only see two seats," Lisa said. "I don't think Rusty will want to share his space."

"If you ladies don't mind sharing the same seat, it's a short drive, and I'll make the sacrifice of sharing the seat worth your while," Terry offered.

Lisa laughed. "From what Joanna told me, I can look forward to an epicurean's delight."

Joanna took Rusty for a short walk, then everyone piled into the Healey. All the way to the turn-off, Lisa described the different delectable chocolates she would bring to what she referred to as the recapture event. But when they reached the lot, they saw John coming out of the apothecary. It was apparent that he was in a hurry by the way he ran upstairs to the apartment.

Terry climbed out and called to Rusty, who immediately ran around to Joanna's side when she got out. She entered the apothecary, Terry two steps ahead of her.

Mack was kneeling over the bloodied form of Bud. Joanna gasped, ran to his side, and squatted down.

"Mack, what happened?"

He rocked back onto his butt. "Kid's all right. Just took a knock to the head."

"But what about all the blood?"

"It's not blood," he responded, making Joanna sigh in relief.

John ran up with a sheet and began tearing into long strips, handing them to Mack.

"Look here," Mack said, wiping at Bud's exposed stomach with one of the sheet strips.

Letters in red felt pen were written across Bud's stomach. "'Get out," Mack read aloud. "Last night you said that the threats would become more intense and frequent." He looked at the assembled group. "It's begun."

Joanna was furious and could feel her ears burn as her eyes filled with unshed tears of anger. She felt a strong-arm wrap around her waist and looked up into Terry's serious face.

"How did this happen?" Terry asked. "Someone came in here and attacked Bud?"

Mack stood. "John and I were working on the deck when we heard a car on the gravel. We figured you were returning and came up. The lot was empty, and Bud was lying in a puddle of that red stuff—tomato sauce and paint or something."

"So," Terry said, "our killer is getting desperate, bold. We've hooked the big fish. Now, all we have to do is reel him in."

Bud groaned, slowly regaining consciousness. The rest looked on as John helped Bud stand. "Let's get you outside into the fresh air," he said as he walked the teen out of the apothecary. "Can you tell us what happened?"

Bud reached a hand up and touched the back of his head. "I heard a noise, like footsteps or something, and before I could turn, I was clubbed."

Mack stepped up and parted the boy's hair for a close look at the bump. "Whoever it was, they didn't want to kill you."

"What do you mean?" Joanna interjected.

"The strike to the head rendered Bud unconscious. If he'd been allowed to fall, the force of his head hitting the cement floor probably would have killed him."

"What? So we have a compassionate murderer," John said.

Terry looked around. "We've got two days. No one goes it alone."

Chapter Forty-five

When Joanna and Terry walked back to the car, Lisa was still sitting in the Healey. "All clear," Terry told her.

Lisa got out and nervously looked around. "I am so sorry," Lisa said. "When I saw all that blood, well, I couldn't just stand around."

"Ladies, I'm afraid that a demonstration of my chef-like abilities are meant for a happy occasion. But I've got the ingredients for my chili that's to die for."

Lisa delivered a playful punch to Terry's shoulder. "I'll take a rain check. Right now, I'd like to go home and lock all my doors."

"Sure, Lisa. I've got no problem taking you home. But honestly," he said, "whoever was behind this attack is not going to track anyone down. You should be perfectly safe." He turned to Joanna. "Joanna, I want you out working on the deck with John and Mack. Bud can kick back in the shade. I'll be back as soon as I drop Lisa off."

It was a cool day, and by noon, a light breeze had come up. Joanna sat with Bud, Rusty at her side, at the back of the apothecary, watching John and Mack work. John would dig holes and spread a couple of inches of gravel, then Mack would set the peer block, six in all. Then, they unloaded lumber from her pickup to a tarp.

After a while, Joanna asked, "Coffee, anyone?"

Both men stopped what they were doing. "Black," they said in unison, then laughed.

Joanna looked at Bud. "How about a beer for you?"

Bud smiled. "Sounds just right."

Rusty followed her up to the apartment and sat next to her as she prepared the coffee.

Bud was leaning against the back of the apothecary when he felt some movement. It took a minute before he realized that the dumbwaiter was moving.

"Hey guys, I think Joanna is coming down in the dumbwaiter.

I'm going to go give her a hand."

Mack stood and gave him a wave. "There and back. No detours."

Bud waved back.

Joanna was pulling three mugs from the cupboard when she heard the dumbwaiter and figured John or Mack was coming up to help, but when she turned, it was to face a black-clad figure pointing a gun at her.

"You should never have come to Dungeness Bay."

The figure raised the gun and pointed it at Joanna's chest. That's when Rusty charged.

At the sound of a gunshot, Bud froze. Mack and John were jolted into action. Mack ran up the steps and John went for Joanna's gun in the Ural, then sprinted up the steps, taking them two at a time.

Mack barreled into the apartment, expecting to take fire.

"Here, in here," Joanna yelled.

Mack ran toward the kitchen but paused to follow a trail of blood that led to the dumbwaiter. "John, they're getting away in the dumbwaiter!"

Gun in hand, John spun around and bounded down the steps.

When Mack entered the kitchen, Joanna was leaning against the wall, her legs splayed out, Rusty's head resting on her lap.

"Mack, take my truck. Find Stan! Rusty has been shot," Joanna said urgently.

"Pack the wound with ice and keep him still," Mack yelled as he ran out of the apartment.

When John entered the apothecary, he found Bud unconscious again. There was no blood, but Bud would be getting another goose egg.

Twenty minutes later, Stan's bike roared across the gravel parking lot, Mack on his tail with the truck.

"Upstairs," Mack said. "She's in the kitchen."

As Stan ran up, Mack heard a moan and stepped around the truck. John and Bud were sitting on the grass on the edge of the gravel, leaning against a tree.

"What do you think?" Mack said.

"The one that struck old Bud here," John said, "never left. That's why we didn't see a car. They had hidden in the dumbwaiter."

"I'd say they were planning on taking Joanna out."

John held up the gun. "I'm fine here. You go on up and check on Joanna and the dog."

Mack had just entered the apartment when John heard a car coming down the driveway. He nudged Bud around to the far side of the tree and then raised the gun, figuring he'd take out the driver. But when an Austin-Healey came into sight, he rested the gun on his leg. The Healey skidded sideways to a halt in the gravel. Terry scrambled out and ran to John's side.

"What happened?"

"Our killer never left. They came up the dumbwaiter after Joanna. Bud just got in the way, but he'll be fine."

Terry, who had sprinted toward and up the steps as soon as Mack mentioned the killer trying to take out Joanna, didn't hear the last part about Bud.

He burst into the apartment and followed the voices to the kitchen. Joanna was leaning on the counter. Stan was bent over Rusty.

"Joanna?"

She ran into his open arms. "Oh God, Terry. The murderer came up the dumbwaiter, said I never should have come to Dungeness Bay and would have shot me if Rusty hadn't charged him."

Stan stood and came over. "I've got him sedated. The bullet trimmed the skin off the top of his head and caught him again just above the tail. He'll be fine, but judging from the blood, skin, and cloth in his mouth and the trail of blood leading to the dumbwaiter, I'd say he got his pound of flesh, so to speak. He'll be out for about an hour."

Mack walked up. "Place is clean."

Joanna took Terry's hand. "Let's go down and check on Bud."

Stan followed, medical bag in hand. He and Mack played twenty questions with the teen, then Stan finally pulled some pills from his bag, saying, "Take these."

Bud made a face.

"Hey, don't worry," Stan said. "I keep them in my bag for me when I've had a rough day."

Joanna ran a hand through her hair. "Things have spiraled out of control, but we need to stay firm with the plan."

"That's an understatement," Mack said. "I'd say this whole business has gone way beyond out of control." He said and looked sternly at Joanna. "Someone just tried to kill you, and we still have two days before the investigator gets here and we can trap the murderer."

"Please," Joanna said, "if we falter now, this will be for nothing."

Chapter Forty-six

Terry pulled Joanna to one side, then turned to face the others. "Time for a change of plans. The apothecary is no longer safe. I'll take Bud and Joanna to my place and bring Joanna back for her tai chi class tomorrow."

Mack looked over at John. "Sounds good. I'll lock up the apothecary and we'll camp out in the apartment. Snow should be back in the woods tonight, and the three of us will lock the place down."

Joanna felt taken care of but, at the same time, out of control. There was no doubt in her mind that Bud needed to be out of harm's way, in a quiet and safe place to recuperate. But where would this leave her?

They rolled Rusty onto a blanket and, with the help of Stan, Mack, and John, got him down the stairs and into the back of the Austin-Healey. Stan gave Joanna a bag of painkillers and a bottle of sedatives to give Rusty at night to make sure he slept. Bud squeezed in by climbing on Joanna's lap, and they were off.

Terry lived in a one-story, three-bedroom house with an attached garage. When they arrived, Terry parked in the driveway, ran up, and opened the front door, then helped Joanna and Bud lug Rusty, who was still sedated, out of the Healey and into the house. Once inside, they set him down for a rest.

"Let's take him into the room at the end of the hall," Terry said. "Joanna, this will also be your room. I think you should be near if he wakes up."

On the count of three, they picked up the blanket and hundred pounds of sleeping dog. They stumbled down the hall, staggered into the bedroom, and lay him at the foot of the bed. The three quietly stepped into the hall, leaving the door open, then followed Terry into the kitchen.

"Guess what we're having for dinner?"

Joanna walked over to the refrigerator and peered inside at the large pot of chili, then shut the door. "Let me guess—chili?"

Terry smiled. "And garlic bread and beer."

During dinner, Bud consumed three bottles of beer. He seemed to not be in pain but remained seated while Joanna and Terry cleared the table. All three then moved into the living room.

"You'll find linens, pillows, and blankets in the closets. The bathroom is at the end of the hall. Another beer, anyone?"

Terry and Joanna were surprised when Bud declined.

Joanna was relieved to have her own room. She had a special feeling for Terry that was growing with his every deed, but she wasn't ready to sleep with him.

"I hate to desert you two," Bud said, "but I took those painkillers that Stan gave me and combined with the beer, man are they knocking me out. If I don't make the bed up now, I'll be sleeping on a bare mattress."

Terry walked back into the kitchen and started washing the dishes. Joanna looked around. "You got a dish towel?"

"Third drawer down, next to the fridge."

They washed and dried in silence. Then Terry dried his hands and brought out two more beers. "Let's head into the living room."

This was Joanna's third beer, and she was beginning to feel it. For just a moment, she wished she was back in her apartment with Rusty and her journal, then she relaxed and let her mind wander to where the night would take her. She slowly faded into a deep sleep.

. . . .

When Joanna woke up, she gave a little laugh. It was morning and she was in her underwear, in bed under the covers, alone. She took a quick look around the room and spotted her clothes, including her shoes, on a chair, and no sign of Rusty. She quickly dressed and stepped out into the hall.

Rusty was just off the hall in the living room. His eyes were open. He whined when he saw her but didn't get up. She got down on her hands and knees and crawled over to him, making all sorts of happy sounds, then stroked one of his paws. "You saved my life, big guy. Once you're off the medications, there'll be double rations of kibble for you."

Terry walked in and said, "Hey, how did you sleep?"

Joanna stood, walked over, and kissed Terry on the lips, then stepped back. "I slept well, but there was, however, the matter of my undressed state."

Terry didn't miss a beat. "You were out minutes after what I think was your fourth beer. I took the opportunity to make up your bed, then pulled you into a fireman's carry and flopped you down on the bed. I simply removed anything that might bind and left the necessities in place."

"Well, thank you for that," she said. She stepped forward and gave him another kiss, holding it just a little bit longer, but pulled away when she felt his hands begin to caress her sides.

"Hey, you two, what's for breakfast?"

"How are you feeling Bud?" Joanna asked.

"Knowing what I went through, not bad, actually. A few tender spots, but really not bad."

"Think you can get back to work on the chest?" Terry asked.

Bud gave his head a little dip. "I'm more determined than ever to finish it."

"That's my man," Joanna said. "Let's head back and I'll fix a big breakfast for everyone."

They managed to lure Rusty out of the house with a handful of kibble. When they pulled back the passenger seat, he climbed in and flopped down.

It was a twenty-minute drive from Terry's house to the apothecary. When they got out of the Healey, they could clearly hear hammers pounding and low chatter, but it abruptly stopped. A minute later, Stan and Snow came around one side and Mack and John, with his gun, came from the opposite side.

"Hey guys," Terry said.

Snow smiled. He walked forward, shook Terry's hand, and introduced himself, then turned and gave Joanna a friendly hug. "The guys filled me in. I'm glad to see you're all right." He looked over at Bud. "You too."

"We've got a surprise for you," Stan said.

Rusty managed to get out of the car with a lot of "good boys" and kibble, but once out, he just lay in the shadow of the front tire.

"What surprise?"

"We've been working since first light," Mack said.

Joanna, Terry, and Bud followed the four men around the corner.

A big grin appeared on Joanna's face. "My deck. You finished my deck."

Chapter Forty-seven

They all climbed up on the deck and John gave a small tour. "We still need to put railings along the front, so you and your students won't fall off the bluff, and where we just climbed up, there'll be three long steps. The entire deck has to be sealed but we can do that tomorrow. Today's class shouldn't hurt anything."

"I can't thank you all enough," Joanna said.

"I have a surprise, too," Bud added.

Every head turned to face the teen, who was grinning. "It's in the apothecary."

They followed him around until he got to the entrance and stopped.

"Lisa Posey told me that you have a line of teas and that you made some Chinese five-spice chocolate truffles. If you open the door, I'll show you what I made."

Joanna did. The table that she saw was counter-high with slots created by slanted cheery wood slats. "These will hold the tea bags," Bud pointed out. "The wood is sealed and stained and thinly coated with varathane. Here," he indicated a longboard that lay on the tabletop, "is for the truffles or muffins. It can all be soaked or scrubbed."

Delighted, Joanna walked over and gave Bud a kiss on the cheek.

"Hey," John protested. "We built a deck. Where's our kiss?"

They all laughed, and Joanna blushed.

"I could kiss you all," she said gratefully.

The sound of tires on the gravel made the group grow somber and cautious. They collectively sighed a breath of relief when they saw Lisa Posey getting out of her SUV.

"Well, don't just stand there staring. Someone give me a hand. I've got three dozen five-spice truffles," she said, and walked up and looked at Bud. "Did you finish the display?" He nodded.

Joanna couldn't believe this was all coming together. "My teas are still packed in their water-tight container."

"You go get them," Lisa said. "We'll set out the truffles. I also brought some paper cups."

While Joanna was up in the apartment, Terry looked at the other men. "What are you guys thinking for security?"

"I'm going back into the woods," Snow said. "We're bringing a couple of sawhorses out with some boards for Stan to work on. Mack will hang out around the deck like he's taking measurements for the steps. John, since he's got the gun, will be in the apothecary, and the apartment will be locked, with Bud inside."

"Sounds perfect," Terry said. "As for me, I'll be taking my first tai chi lesson and then mixing with the class when they break for refreshments."

Mack motioned Bud forward and held out his hand, with a pencil eraser-sized dot on his palm. "This, my friend, is a throat mic." He placed the dot on the side of his throat and then passed out earbuds to everyone else.

"Okay Bud, all you have to do is touch the mic. You don't have to speak. Just touch, and it'll send out a signal of static to all the earbuds. If somebody so much as rattles the door, you touch that mic and we'll come running. Now test it out and give us a buzz."

Bud did, and everyone gave a thumbs up.

Joanna came down the stairs clutching a small box. "You aren't going to desert me, are you?"

"Not a chance," Terry said.

"Good to hear," Joanna said. "Students should start arriving in about half an hour."

While they waited, Joanna and Lisa fussed over the display, complimenting Bud on his work.

Terry stepped close. "I'll be taking part in your class. The others will be scattered, but we'll all be watching."

"What about Bud?"

"He'll be up in your apartment with the door locked and a throat mic that connects to all of us."

. . . .

The class of seven turned into twelve, and the forty-by-twenty-foot deck was just the right size. This time, only two were tourists, neither of whom had any experience. Joanna couldn't help but notice that Terry seemed to excel during the exercises and moved smoothly through each form. After half an hour and twenty repetitions, the class broke up. Most walked over to the display, eager to try the chocolate truffles. Terry hung back with those who just sat on the deck, gazing out to sea.

By ten o'clock, the last person had left, and the class had gone off without a hitch. Only three of the truffles remained and everyone wanted to know how they could get more of Joanna's tea.

When Joanna knocked on her locked apartment door, she was taken completely by surprise when all four men came roaring up the steps. When they told her that Bud must have pressed his throat mic, she laughed and pounded on the door.

"Bud, it's me. Open up."

Throughout the day, Rusty hadn't moved, and though he once again had to be coaxed, made it up the steps on his own.

The apothecary was locked up after Lisa went home. Mack, John, and Snow remained on the grounds, mainly working on the steps and the rail.

Terry pulled Bud to one side. "Joanna has become a target. I'll be taking her to my bar for lunch then bringing her back to the apartment to go over tomorrow's plan, and then I'm taking her home. John and Mack will be staying in the apartment with you tonight."

"What are you guys whispering about?"

Terry turned to face Joanna. "Just going over tomorrow's plan. Right now, I'm taking you to lunch. I figure we'll all meet in the afternoon to go over the plans for our trap for the last time."

Joanna asked, "Bud, are you okay with this?"

Bud nodded. "I'm locking up the apartment, then I'll take the dumbwaiter down to finish up the chest and put together the strongbox."

"All right. I'll see you later this afternoon."

When she climbed in the Austin-Healey, Terry didn't start the engine until she was buckled up. She noticed that he was driving a little slower than usual.

As they headed for the bar and grill, Terry said, "Joanna, I really enjoy your company and I know it's been surrounded by a stressful situation. But after this is all behind you, I'd like to continue to see you."

Chapter Forty-eight

Lunch was a bowl of chili—big surprise there—and when they finished, Terry drove Joanna to Whaler's Beach, where the two just sat and watched the breakers pummel the stones and formations just beyond the surf. When the afternoon breeze picked up, she slid next to him and closed her eyes, breathing in his scent.

"Terry, my husband passed just six months ago, and I just don't know if I'm ready for a relationship."

He leaned down and kissed her. "I know, and I know you've been through a lot since you arrived in Dungeness Bay. All I ask is that you think about it. I'm here for you whatever you decide."

She kissed him, and they got up and went back to the Healey and rode in silence to the apothecary. When he parked, he took her hand to keep her from getting out.

"It still isn't safe here for you tonight. Come back to my place. Stay in the same room—no strings attached. I'm just not letting you out of my sight until the killer is arrested."

She gave his hand a squeeze. "Thank you."

That evening, the plan was rehearsed until everyone knew where everyone else would be. Joanna stressed to Mack and John that the intention was to trap the killer, who would be in possession of the fake map, at which time he would be arrested by either Sheriff Cowdrey or the DA's agent. But a direct confrontation was the last resort.

Tension was high for Joanna, not just because in the next twenty-four hours, the murderer of Gus and Thayer would be under arrest, but also because she would have to deal with the investigator sent on behalf of the state district attorney.

After their discussion, Terry went to help Bud with the construction of the metal strongbox and John and Mack resumed working on the deck steps.

Joanna was on the patch of grass next to the parking area doing her tai chi when a car pulled up and parked to one side of the apothecary entrance. Terry and Bud walked to the edge of the apothecary and watched as a young man in a suit and tie climbed out of his BMW and walked up to Joanna. He observed Joanna moving through her last forms. When she finished, she turned to face him. "Can I help you with something?"

"Yes, I'm Doug Lemon from the district attorney's office. I'm looking for Joanna Bright."

Having just finished her tai chi, Joanna felt centered and grounded. "I'm Joanna Bright. I wasn't expecting you until tomorrow."

He smiled. "Well then, I guess today I'm here unofficially. This is a sweet assignment. I'm usually in my office or the state courthouse in Salem, so I just couldn't resist coming down early."

Joanna hid her relief. This man wasn't what she expected at all. She caught Terry's gaze and gave a happy wave.

"I'd like to talk to you about what's been going on, if that would be all right?"

"Even though I'm not really here today, and my official capacity begins tomorrow, I caution you that everything you say could bias me in one direction or another."

"Then let me start by asking what you're hoping to accomplish with this visit."

"Fair enough. As you are probably aware, the former sheriff of Dungeness Bay, Jesse Collins, submitted a file to my office describing events surrounding the death of Gus Hasselbacker, and in that report, he named you as the sole person of interest. I'm here to determine the validity of that assertion."

"That's all I needed to know. I know this great bar and grill that serves chili to die for, where I can fill you in on events and how I would like to involve you in the capture of the real murderer of Gus Hasselbacker.

At the mention of the *real* murderer, Doug started. "You're on."

"We can take my truck."

Twenty minutes later, Doug scraped the inside of his bowl with his spoon for the last dregs of chili. He pushed the empty dish aside, picked up his mug of beer, and took a long drink.

"You were right. That chili was by far the best I've ever had. As to the events that have occurred over the past week, as you've described them, I confess that I'm amazed that you're sitting here at all, let alone as calm as you are. I would have hightailed it back to Monterey. That aside, even in my official capacity, I'm here only to gather facts and take some conclusions back to Salem with me. I can't make an arrest, and although I can give your plan my personal stamp of approval, I can only witness an event. I can in no way intervene. As an employee of the state district attorney's office, I'm not even allowed to make a citizen's arrest."

"Then you'll take your assigned place in the apothecary tomorrow night?" Joanna pressed.

"What you're asking me to do is out of the purview of the DA's office, but yes. I wouldn't miss the opportunity to witness the capture and arrest of this killer for the world. I am, however, required to get permission from the sheriff to be present. But believe me, I won't have any problem convincing him that my presence will be a feather in his cap and that his cooperation will appear on my report."

Chapter Forty-nine

A dark figure wearing camouflage crept silently through the dense forest of poplar and red elder trees, walking, stopping to listen, then moving on. Darkness prevailed over the moonless night. When the figure reached the tent, they paused to remove a tiny syringe, and then entered the shelter. Their breathing slowed and sensory perception dominated their situational awareness until they located the sleeping form of William Snow. The needle was held over the exposed ankle for a second, then plunged through the thin epidermal layer of skin through which less than a drop of the paralyzing syrup from the South American poplar tree was dispersed. William Snow felt something less biting than a mosquito.

The shadowy figure moved around the parameter of the parking area, careful not to step onto the gravel, then down to the beach, invisible to the two women marching back and forth, up the bluff to the back side of the apothecary, and then along the bare ground to the steps that led to Joanna's apartment and the dumbwaiter within.

The big doors of the apothecary, including the metal storm doors, were closed and locked. The only way in was down the dumbwaiter from Joanna's apartment.

John lay in Joanna's bed, and Mack was in the spare bedroom. Down in the apothecary Doug Lemon sat in the shadows just ten feet from the special stand that held the wooden chest that contained the metal strongbox. Terry watched over the back door, and Joanna and Bud covered the dumbwaiter.

When John heard the door of the apartment open, he touched his throat mic, sending a single blip of static to Joanna's ear, signaling that someone had entered.

Hearing the dumbwaiter car moving, Joanna elbowed Bud, who touched his throat mic, sending a signal of static to the ear of Doug Lemon.

Doug had made it clear that if someone broke into the apothecary, they would have to be allowed to take the chest or the metal box out. The plan was that once the dumbwaiter's car was at the bottom of the shaft in the apothecary, Mack and John would join Snow in the forest to stop the suspect from getting away. At the top of the driveway, Eric Ward had parked his truck, blocking that exit. Bobby Alvarez and Lisa Posey watched the beach.

The figure climbed into the dumbwaiter and descended into the apothecary. Joanna elbowed Bud and pointed to the door of the dumbwaiter. He nodded and moved deeper into the shadows.

The door opened, revealing a small figure dressed in black and wearing a face cover. The figure remained still, crouching in the dumbwaiter car. A full minute passed before the figure stepped out of the little car.

Joanna watched the figure approach the chest. Something about the way the intruder moved looked familiar—short, quick steps. She flashed on her visit to the Outpouring coffee shop. Joanna sucked in a breath. The height was right, and the quick steps matched. Could Cheryl Chin be the killer of Gus and Thayer? She had a thriving business. Was twenty-five million her rationale for murder?

With all the stealth she could muster, Joanna stepped out of the shadows, moving until she stood diagonally behind the figure.

"Cheryl?"

The figure spun, pulling a gun in the process. "You should have left when you had the chance."

Bud felt paralyzed. He was afraid that if he moved, Cheryl would shoot Joanna. Doug was in the shadows at an angle and couldn't see what was going on but could hear the conversation.

"Why, Cheryl?"

"Why? Reparation for all the wrongs my people endured, for the exclusion act that wouldn't allow my grandparents to own a business. Something I vowed to do."

"Yes, and you did," Joanna said. "You own and operate a successful business."

"At first, I thought that was enough. Like everyone else in Dungeness Bay, I knew the story of the miners' gold, but I knew it was true.

Doctors Ing Hay and Long On didn't dare reveal that they were operating a profitable business."

"But murder?" Joanna protested.

"Not murder, reparation. All I needed was the manuscript. It told of three possible locations." Cheryl looked over at the metal chest on its wood display stand. "But you got to it first."

"Where was the gold? Tell me where you found it. Tell me, I need to know." Cheryl's voice was shrill as she walked to the chest. "This must be a sample. Is it gold dust and nuggets?"

"I didn't find the gold. There's nothing in the chest."

Cheryl pushed the chest off its stand and opened the strongbox. "Rocks," she screamed, and lurched to her feet, taking aim at Joanna's chest. "Last chance. Where's the gold?"

Out of the shadows, Sheriff Cowdrey lurched forward, forcing the gun arm up, but was too late. A single shot struck Joanna in the center of the chest. Then she wrestled her gun arm free.

Doug lurched out of the shadows and was shot.

Bud dropped to his hands and knees and crawled past Doug to the still figure of Joanna. He looked up at the sound of a struggle and saw someone being thrown into a stack of boxes that were sitting on several shelves. He saw Cheryl aim and fire widely, causing Sheriff Cowdrey to take a bullet in the shoulder.

Cheryl scrambled back into the dumbwaiter car, closed the door, and began pulling herself up.

Bobby Alvarez and Lisa Posey had come up from the beach when they heard the gun shot, but found the back door locked. Together, they picked up a four by four and, like a battering ram, knocked the door open. Lisa paused, picked up a short length of two by four, and then ran in to find Bobby struggling with a man at least a foot taller. Without a sound, Lisa walked up and struck the man on the back of the head.

It was Bobby who had spotted the man coming down the ladder from the loft. When he had stepped down to the floor, she had stepped out. He raised his gun, then crumpled to the ground as Lisa stood over him, 2x4 in hand, ready, in case he tried to get up. He didn't move. The two women charged forward when they saw a figure leaning over Joanna.

Bud stood up, waving his hands. "It's just Terry. Joanna's been shot."

They stopped, and Bud turned when both big apothecary doors opened.

Alex Jenner stood in the doorway, shotgun in hand. He looked around the room expectantly, then his gaze settled on Joanna's still figure and Terry.

He waved the barrel at Liza and Bobby. "You two. Move next to Terry. This is going to look like a robbery gone terribly wrong. The intruder wanted the gold but realized there was no gold. So he goes bonkers and kills you all," Alex said. He raised the shotgun to his hip. A shot rang out, and he spiraled to the floor.

Chapter Fifty

Bobby, Lisa, and Bud rushed up next to Terry, who was pulling off Joanna's sweatshirt.

"Thank God she decided to wear the bulletproof vest." All heads turned to look at Cowdrey, who looked over at Doug. "You too."

"All state vehicles have one in the trunk," Doug said.

Terry stood and held a hand behind one ear. "Hear that? It's Rusty. Bud, stay with Joanna."

Terry lunged and took the gun from Doug. He ran out the front of the apothecary and up the stairs, shouldered open the apartment door, and ran in, following the sound of the growl.

Rusty had chased after Cheryl Chin, who was cowering on the writing desk. Moments later, Sheriff Cowdrey and Doug made their way up the steps and joined Terry.

Cowdrey's right arm was hanging limp and he was pale as a ghost. "Terry, call off Rusty and restrain him. Cheryl, climb down." As soon as he got his last word out, he passed out. Doug caught him on the way to the floor and took the handcuffs from his belt, walking over and cuffing Cheryl's hands behind her back. He urged her into the dumbwaiter, where he pushed her into the little car, lowered it halfway to the apothecary, and locked it in place.

Terry left Doug to stay with the unconscious sheriff and ran back downstairs, where he found Lisa and Bobby on each side of the now-conscious Joanna, walking her around the parking lot.

. . . .

The next day, Terry hung the closed sign on the window of his bar and grill. Inside, Joanna, Lisa, and Bobby sat across from Doug Lemon and Sheriff Cowdrey. Bud sat on a rug with Rusty.

Doug clinked his empty beer mug with a spoon to stop the chatter.

Joanna looked around the table. "I can't believe that John,

Mack, and Alex were behind the murders. And Cheryl, oh my God."

"I was up interrogating Cheryl most of the night," Doug said. "It seems that Alex came to Dungeness Bay to help Gus Hasselbacker financially. Gus convinced him to invest in a condominium project. Apparently, the permits were denied, and Gus lost his shirt in the deal. That's when Gus, who had been working with writer Thayer Spelling, said he knew where the miners' gold was located. But he didn't really know and was just bidding his time until Spelling's research revealed the location.

"When he was confronted by Alex, he confessed that he didn't really know the location, and Alex flew into a rage and killed Gus. That's about the time you arrived, Joanna, and found his body. But it was all for nothing. Gus was desperate and had told Alex that he knew the location, thinking that he just had to get Spelling to tell him. When he found out that she didn't know either, he killed her."

Dough's narrative was interrupted when Eric walked in with a groggy-looking William Snow. He pulled a couple of chairs over to the long table where everyone was sitting.

Eric looked at the faces sitting around the table. "I'd swung the truck around when I heard the gunshots, then Snow staggered out into the middle of the driveway. I packed him in the truck and hightailed it to Stan's place."

He continued, "He may be a veterinarian, but he did wonders for my dizzy spells, and gave something to Snow to bring him out of his stupor."

"Glad the two of you made it," Doug said. "I was just explaining the interrogation with Cheryl Chin."

"How did Cheryl get involved?" Joanna questioned.

"Alex knew something of her resentment over the treatment of her grandparents and convinced her that if she could scare you into leaving, he and two friends could find the gold and would cut her in. But when her notes didn't scare you off, Alex stepped in. He was the one who cut the brake line on the Ural. Meanwhile, John and Mack were hanging around, ready to act if you discovered the location of the gold."

"What about the rail on the loft giving way? Alex couldn't have faked that fall," Joanna said.

"Cheryl said she didn't know anything about that. But I'm fairly sure that John and Mack were trying to get rid of Alex. When he survived, they had to do everything they could to stay close to you and gain your confidence. That's why they moved him in to recuperate."

Doug looked over at Lisa and Bobby. "Which one of you took out John and Mack?"

Lisa raised her hand like a schoolgirl, grinning ear to ear. "When I saw Bobby in trouble, well, he got the worst of it."

"That would be John," Sheriff Cowdrey said.

"The guy was a bull," Terry added. "He knocked me to the floor, but I threw him head over heels with an ippon seoi nage."

"Oh yeah," Bud exclaimed. "I saw him fly into a bunch of boxes."

Cowdrey nodded and looked at Lisa. "You caught him on the occipital lobe with that two-by-four. He's still out; Mack wasn't much better off." He smiled. "At least he could walk and was easy to manage. Johns still hogtied in the apothecary, and Alex is dead," Cowdrey looked over at Doug, "thanks to deadeye here. My right arm down to my fingers was out of commission."

"What will happen to Cheryl?" Joanna asked.

"She claims to have done nothing more than writing those notes," Doug said.

"Bull," Joanna said. "She would have shot me if not for Rusty. She shot my dog. That has to count for something."

"Cheryl has a lot to account for," Doug said, "thanks to Sheriff Cowdrey's quick thinking." He gave Cowdrey and Eric a nod. "The Sheriff requested Helen Ward be contacted. She came in to witness the interrogation. There's no way that Cheryl can claim any kind of harassment or verbal abuse, or that I forced a confession."

Joanna could feel herself clouding up. "I was such a fool, taken in by Alex, John, and Mack."

"Don't feel bad," Lisa said. "John and Mack had us all fooled."

Joanna nodded and thought to herself how Alex had even Doc Hay fooled.

"They took me in," Snow said. "They used me. My presence legitimized theirs."

"But why were they going to kill us?" Joanna said. "How would that get them any closer to the gold? After all, they were all in on the plan."

Chapter Fifty-one

Bud got up, walked over to Joanna, and put his hand on her shoulder. "Alex, by reading Thayer's manuscript, determined the three possible locations of the gold, but as long as Joanna was hanging around, he couldn't check them out. He got Cheryl to write the notes, and when that didn't work, he tried cutting your brake line. It came down to having to clear the deck and set up John and Mack to help in the process, convincing Cheryl that all she had to do was break into the apothecary and get the map, even though he knew it to be fake.

"However, the showdown turned out, he would show up take out the survivors, including John and Mack, making Cheryl the fall guy, and in the process, clearing the deck. He'd bide his time and then search the three locations."

Bobby picked up the narrative. "Alex probably figured, and rightly so, that after all the bloodshed around the apothecary, the mayor would probably have it torn down, replacing it with a park. At that point, he'd be free to search the three locations."

Bud leaned forward and picked up a spoon from the table, clicking it against Joanna's empty beer mug to recapture everyone's attention. "I know where the gold is buried," he declared.

"What?" Joanna said. "How?"

"Elementary deduction. The three locations were the apothecary itself, the smokehouse, and the Chinese cemetery. I eliminated the apothecary when I found the hidden compartment with the gold ledger. The simplest place to hide the gold, and Thayer Spelling's first choice, would be the smokehouse. With decades of ashes, it would have been a simple matter to dump the gold in the ash pit."

"That leaves the Chinese cemetery," Eric said. "But there are hundreds of graves. We can't dig them all up."

Bud walked to the door. "Meet me at the Chinese graveyard and bring some shovels." He pushed through the door, walked across the parking lot, and climbed in his Karmann Ghia.

The group exited the bar in time to watch him drive off, then followed.

Terry climbed in the cab next to Joanna. "What do you think?"

"I have no idea what Bud's up to, but I've got two shovels in the shed."

Twenty minutes later, they were all gathered in the cemetery around Bud, who was sitting in a chair next to an aging Chinese man in a wheelchair. A young Asian woman stood nearby.

"Remember when I told you that I had a translator for the gold ledger?" Bud asked Joanna.

Joanna nodded.

"I'd like you all to meet Long On's grandson," Bud said, helping the old man stand. "I'll let him explain."

"My grandfather held no animosity toward the anti-Chinese sentiment of the time and left the apothecary to the town of Dungeness Bay. He also wanted to leave the gold to the community but knew the time wasn't right. And so, he had my father—his son—promise that he would be buried with the gold. In a series of dreams, my grandfather's partner, Ing Hay, came to me. In one such dream, he announced that a woman with a great high spirit, a protector of our legacy who would meet many challenges, had come to live in the apothecary, signaling that the time was right to reveal the fruits of our labor."

The old man sat down hard, and, in response, the Asian woman stepped forward.

"Grandpa, are you ready to go home?" He nodded, and she wheeled him toward a van.

"The gold is here," Bud said. "Mister On requested that the mayor be present when it's dug up and that it must be distributed in such a manner that will allow Dungeness Bay to flourish for all time."

Ten days later, Bud sat between Bobby and Lisa, who was seated next to Terry and Joanna, Rusty at her feet. In a second row of chairs were Eric and Helen, Stan, Sheriff Cowdrey, Doug, who was there representing the state of Oregon, and the mayor.

The ceremony was short. The mayor thanked Long On's grandson, who sat in a wheelchair next to his granddaughter in a place of honor. The soil was broken, but the actual retrieval of the gold took two days.

At the end of the ceremony, Joanna invited everyone to the apothecary for a meal to celebrate the life of the two Chinese doctors. Terry prepared the main course and Lisa provided more Chinese five-spice chocolate truffles.

While everyone was raving over the food and rehashing the events that had led to the discovery of the gold, Joanna went down into the basement.

"Doc?" Joanna called out.

"I am here."

"Did you know of the ceremony honoring you and Long On? Were you able to attend?"

"I'm afraid I could not attend. It took place beyond my borders. I, however, was informed by my old friend, Long On, who appeared and regaled me with all that took place. Then, he disappeared."

"I don't understand."

"He was somehow assigned to protect the gold until it was time to be distributed and I was assigned to protect the apothecary until you arrived. With the gold in the hands of the good mayor of Dungeness Bay, my friend's task was complete, and he was freed from this earthly place."

"What of you?"

"Your presence no doubt casts a protective shadow over the apothecary, but there are many challenges ahead that we will face together. Watch over your four-legged friend; he is your true protector. And cherish every moment with your two-legged suitor, who, I believe, is currently on his way here in search of his heart's content."

Then the shimmering image of Doc Hay vanished. A bright light illuminated the stone steps and led Terry to her side.

"Joanna, what are you doing down here?"

She scratched Rusty as he pressed against her leg then turned and wrapped Terry in a hug. "Just waiting for you."

Keep reading for a special excerpt from the next exciting Joanna Bright Dungeness Bay cozy murder mystery series.

Double Exposure

Prologue

Jake Harvey nervously cleaned up the gas station's office then moved

to the garage, putting away tools that had strayed and wiping up oil spills. He looked around and gave his head a shake. Jupiter Discount Gas hadn't made him rich but had paid for his house and kept him comfortable. Now, with the right decision, it would keep him that way for years to come.

He wasn't surprised when Myron Allen stepped into the garage. Jake knew he'd have to face him, sooner than later.

"Hello, Jake. I brought the papers," Myron said.

"I changed my mind," Jake said. "I've pulled my gas station off the market."

Myron reached into his inside coat pocket and pulled out a check.

"Sign the papers, and this check for five hundred thousand dollars is yours, right now. Deposit it today."

Jake stepped over one of the arms of the auto lift to glance at the check, still considering the sale, then shook his head. "My mind's made up, Myron. I'm just not ready to sell the station."

Myron was desperate, he'd put a deposit down on the wrecking crew that would tear down the old service station and lined up a contractor who would begin work on the condominiums within the week. He stepped up and waved the check in Jake's face in frustration.

"Take the check, Jake. You agreed to make the sale last week and I've moved ahead with plans and promises based on your word."

Jake folded his arms. "My decision is final. Leave Myron. I've got a business to run."

Myron lunged forward and shoved the check into the breast pocket of Jake's work shirt. Jake yanked it out, tore it in half, and threw it on the cement floor.

"Damn you!" Myron shouted as he closed the distance and straight-armed Jake, who stumbled backward, tripping over an arm of the hoist. Flailing his arms, Jake fell hard, butt-first, feeling his vertebrae pop. With nothing to grab onto, his right elbow struck the cement and shattered, then his back, then shoulders. Finally, his head collided with the cement. The skull fracture was instantly fatal.

Myron stood frozen, holding his breath. He'd just wanted to jar some sense into him; he had no idea the old man would trip. Then he gasped, ran to the side of the garage, and pulled the chain that closed the big garage door. In a fog of panic, he stumbled back, grabbed Jake by one leg, dragged him to the middle of the lift, and slammed the big red button that raised the lift, and Jake, to the ceiling.

. . . .

Joanna got Rusty, her 100-pound former service dog settled in the bed of the pickup, hooked his leash to a metal clip, then looked up at her apartment door. Still no Bud. She walked around, slid in behind the wheel, and honked the horn.

Bud suddenly appeared, slamming the apartment door shut and running down the stairs, taking the steps two at a time. Joanna leaned over and opened the passenger side door. Bud vaulted in and pulled the door shut. "Sorry, sorry."

"I don't mind dropping you off to get your tools, but I've got an appointment with the manager of the Austin Hayward Gallery. I may be there a while."

Eighteen-year-old Bud Nickels was excited. Joanna had offered him her spare bedroom in exchange for working around the apothecary and repairing an old outbuilding she said he could use as a workshop.

"Do you really think you can turn the old apothecary living quarters into a darkroom?" Joanna asked.

Bud buckled his shoulder harness and Joanna started up the driveway.

"I'll get on it first thing, should—only take a couple days."

"Why exactly did Jake let you go?"

Bud lowered his voice. "He's selling the gas station to some real estate developer. But you can't tell anybody."

Joanna pulled onto Dungeness Bay's main drag and looked in her rearview mirror to check on Rusty.

"How can he do that?" Joanna said. "His is the only service station in town!"

"He told me Budget Gas and Diesel is going on the other side of Terry's Bar and Grill, just outside Dungeness Bay proper, so he feels like this might be the right time to sell and retire."

"Did he say what the developer plans on doing with the property?"

"Jake mentioned condominiums."

Joanna pulled into Jupiter Gas and touched Bud's arm. "I shouldn't be more than half an hour."

Bud slid out and turned to face her. "When you come back, pull up to the garage. Jake said he'd help me load the tool chest into your truck."

He shut the door, turned to Rusty, who was leaning over the side of the truck bed, scratched him behind the ears, then watched Joanna drive off.

At the sound of voices, Myron had moved into the office and pushed the glass front door open just enough to see a kid walk up to the garage door. When he stepped back, letting the door shut, he heard the kid pounding on the metal roll-down door.

"Jake, it's Bud."

Myron knew that when the kid didn't get an answer, he'd head for the office. Facing the big glass window, he watched in horror when a police cruiser pulled up to a pump. Heart pounding, adrenaline pumping through his veins, Myron Allen pushed through the office door.

"Officer, officer," Myron said as he pointed at Bud, "there's blood on the floor in the garage and I saw this kid closing the garage door."

Deputy Jerry Riggs pulled loose the leather strip that held his gun in place.

"Sir, I want you to go back into the office." Riggs took a step toward Bud. "Son, I want you to come with me."

Bud, at the officer's insistence, walked ahead, through the office into the garage. "Sir, just stay put," Riggs said to Allen. Then, he urged Bud into the garage.

"I don't see anything." Riggs said as he scanned the garage floor for blood." He soon saw a puddle forming underneath the hoist.

"Do you know where the owner is, son?"

"No, sir."

They walked to the hydraulic post that raised the lift. Without a word, Officer Riggs took three steps back and drew his gun. "Put your hands behind your back."

"What?"

"Just do it."

"Sir, I don't understand?"

Riggs handcuffed Bud, then ran a hand across the teen's shoulder and held it out for him to see.

"How did you get blood on your shirt?" He looked up. "Aw, shit."

Bud looked up, gasped, and shuddered at the sight of Jake's dead eyes. He looked away.

Riggs gave Bud a shake. "How do you lower the lift?"

"The red button by the door."

Chapter One

Joanna pulled around behind the Austin Hayward Gallery and got out of the truck. She hunched down and looked into the driver's side mirror, checking her hair and makeup. She straightened up and pressed a hand down each thigh, smoothing out the wrinkles in her slacks, then walked over to the back door, pushing it open.

Austin Hayward was the only photo gallery in Dungeness Bay. It was sandwiched between the Book Nook and the Outpouring Coffee House and Café.

When Joanna entered the gallery, she was immediately impressed by the quality of the photos, most of the ocean scenes. A heavy-set man who reminded her of the actor Raymond Burr, an actor who played a wheelchair-bound attorney in the old *Ironside* TV series, rolled out from behind a desk.

She extended a hand. "Mr. Sado?"

"Just Sado, please."

He had a very firm grip.

"I'm Joanna Bright. I got your text."

"Yes, of course, the Tai Chi instructor from Monterey. I heard about your adventures with the apothecary treasure and I'm so sad about Alex Jenner. I didn't know him well, but I liked him."

Joanna felt her face flush, and she stared at the floor, not knowing what to say.

"You must be wondering why I asked for this meeting."

Sado spun his wheelchair around and wheeled briskly to his desk, where he removed an envelope from a drawer.

Joanna stood, mesmerized by a photo of a tall ship with tattered rigging, a fractured mast that tilted to port. The ship listed to starboard, seemingly adrift, with no one aboard.

"Photoshop," Sado noted, and rolled around to her side. "One of the patrons of this gallery apparently spotted some of your work in a Carmel studio and heard that you were in Dungeness Bay. I believe this envelope contains a check and the details of the commission."

She took the envelope and removed the contents, folding the check in half without looking at the amount. "Who's your benefactor? There's no name on the letter."

"Honestly, I don't know. His money appears in the gallery's account on a monthly basis. I traced it to a San Francisco bank, but they claimed that the identity of the sender was confidential. I received a letter along with the commission. When you finish the work, you're to bring it to the gallery. My letter provided a phone number I'm to call, and someone will be sent to pick it up. Very mysterious."

Joanna glanced at a giant clock on the wall. "I'm afraid I've got to run, but I'd like to learn more about this mystery man when you have more to share. Thank you, and I'll keep you posted on my progress."

"I'd like that. I'm always here, and my number is on my card."

Joanna climbed back into her pickup, pulled the check from her pocket, and unfolded it. "Ten thousand dollars," she mused aloud. "I hope Bud is as good as his word and can build a dark room for me."

Joanna was less than a mile out of downtown Dungeness Bay when Sheriff Chuck Cowdrey passed her in his cruiser, all lights and sirens. She pulled onto the shoulder of the road and brought an excited Rusty around from the bed of the truck to the passenger's side of the cab, where he immediately calmed down.

Joanna turned into the Jupiter Gas station and parked by the dumpster. Deputy Riggs jogged up to the side of the truck before she could get out.

"Joanna, what are you doing here?"

"I'm here to pick up Bud Nickels. Jake was going to help him load some tools into the back of my truck."

"I'm afraid that's not going to happen. Bud is under arrest for the murder of Jake Harvey."

"What? That's not possible! Can I talk to Bud?"

"I guess that can't hurt, but Deputy Riggs will have to sit in on the conversation. I've called for the medical examiner and a forensics team to come down from Lincoln City; they should be here in half an hour."

Bud was sitting in the back of Riggs's cruiser. The deputy followed Joanna over and opened the door. She turned to Riggs. "Do you mind if he gets out? The three of us could sit on the curb. I think it will be more comfortable than all of us crammed into the back seat?"

"Guess so."

They settled on the curb in front of the office, Bud sandwiched between Deputy Riggs and Joanna.

"Bud, what happened?"

Bud looked like he wanted to cry, but responded, "Nothing. You dropped me off, I walked over and pounded on the garage door, and the next thing I know this guy comes out of the office telling deputy Riggs here that there's a body in the garage, and that he saw me closing the garage door."

"What guy?" Joanna said.

Riggs leaned forward. "After I cuffed Bud and walked him back to the office where I told the man to wait, he was gone."

Sheriff Cowdrey heard the deputy and squatted down in front of the three. "First thing, Riggs: always get a name."

"Could I see where Jake was killed?" Joanna said.

"The scene's still pretty grizzly even though the ambulance has taken the body away, and I can't let you walk around messing up potential evidence. But you can take a look from the office door."

"Thank you."

When Joanna got to the front office door she stopped; there was no black powder on the door handle. "Sheriff Cowdrey, aren't you forgetting something?"

He walked up. "What?"

"Fingerprints, you haven't dusted for fingerprints. They could be Jake's or those of the man that killed him."

Cowdrey rolled his eyes. "I'll ignore your effort to tell me my business. But let's get one thing straight. You're saying that you don't think Bud killed Jake."

"Correct. They were friends. Jake was going to help load Bud's tools into my truck."

"Friends? I understand that Bud was fired."

"Jake was going to sell the gas station, and let Bud go."

"I haven't heard anything about Jake selling the station. Why would he do that?"

"Maybe someone made the right offer," Joanna said, and walked into the office, where another door opened into the garage. What she saw on the floor engaged her memory. Near the lift were two pieces of paper that, in size and shape, reminded her of the check she had gotten from her mystery man.

"Hey, Joanna, you can't go in there," the sheriff protested.

Joanna picked up the two pieces of paper and walked back, handing them to Cowdrey, and said, "I would say someone made Jake a sizable offer, but it wasn't enough."

The sheriff put the two parts of the check together and whistled, "Five hundred thousand dollars."

Joanna went back to scanning the garage for more evidence but turned at the sound of Deputy Riggs slamming through the front office door.

"Dispatch just radioed that you need to call in on a landline ASAP."

Sheriff Cowdrey walked over to the office desk and picked up the handset, then turned and glared at Joanna.

She held both hands up, walked out of the office, and headed back to Bud, who had been placed back in Riggs Cruiser.

A Request—

Thank you for reading *Storm Front,* Book 1 in the Joanna Bright cozy mystery series. If you enjoyed this story, I would really appreciate it if you would leave a review. It lets me know that you liked the story, and motivates me to continue the series. You can leave a review by visiting the sales page where you purchased the book.

Thank you! — Kit

OTHER BOOKS BY KIT CRUMB

Joanna Bright Dungeness Bay Mysteries

Book 1: Storm Front - An Unwelcomed Arrival
Book 2: Double Exposure
Book 3: The Misty Dawn
Book 4: Death in a Dark Place
Book 5: Cargo

Rye and Claire Medical Thriller series

Body Parts
Body of Evidence
The Camp
Sins of the Father
Altered
Rye and Claire and the Terrorists

M: Private Detective series

Retribution
White Slave Treasure
Project Deep Water
Target Golden Gate

Ghost Detective Mystery series

Book 1: Case of the Stolen Infants
Book 2: The Case of a Wolf in Priest's Clothing
Book 3: The Case of the Nursery Rhyme Murders
Book 4: Pool of Tears
Book 5: Death in the Shadows

Urban Legend series

Dream Master
Ghost Forest
The Haunting of Langdon Hall

Theodore Bond Psychological Thriller series

Time Ripper

Non-fiction

Survival Self-Defense
Navigating Mountain Curves on a Motorcycle

About the Author

KIT CRUMB was born with an insatiable curiosity, and interest in adventure, survival, and the natural world. He has led tours of one of the world's largest dry caverns, worked in radio and television, entertained as professional magician, taught fencing, and scuba diving.

Kit holds a black belt in three martial art systems and taught Kenpo and women's self defense for over fifty years through his Black Dragon Dojos in Arizona, California, and Oregon. His stories often reflect aspects of his real-life experiences and his protagonists are often women who are skilled in the martial arts.

Kit lives high in the southern Oregon Cascade Mountain range, with his partner Christine, a book designer, where he writes full-time and manages their cabin for solo writers seeking a creative retreat and solitude.

His popular podcast, *A Darn Good Mystery - Reviews and Interviews* is available through iTunes, Apple podcasts, Spotify, Stitcher, and at www.adarngoodmystery.com.

Contact Kit by email at: owlcreekpress@gmail.com

Made in the USA
Monee, IL
20 May 2024